Copyright © 2021 by Mi

All rights reserved. No part of this text may be reproduced, transmitted, downloaded, decompiled, reverse-engineered, or stored in, or introduced into any information storage and retrieval system, in any form or by any means, whether electronic or mechanical, now known, hereinafter invented, without express written permission of the publisher. For permission requests, write to the publisher, addressed "Attention: Permissions Coordinator," at the address below.

Typewriter Pub, an imprint of Blvnp Incorporated
A Nevada Corporation
1887 Whitney Mesa DR #2002
Henderson, NV 89014
www.typewriterpub.com/info@typewriterpub.com

ISBN: 978-1-64434-143-8

DISCLAIMER
This book is a work of fiction. The characters, incidents, and dialogue are drawn from the author's imagination and are not to be construed as real. While references might be made to actual historical events or existing locations, the names, characters, places, and incidents are either products of the author's imagination or are used fictitiously, and any resemblance to actual persons living or dead, business establishments, events or locales is entirely coincidental.

SAY YOU WON'T LET GO

MIA GOLDING

To Diana,
for being there every step of the way.

Trigger Warning:
*The following story contains scenes and mentions of suicide.
Reader discretion is advised.*

CHAPTER ONE

The worst part about losing someone is losing them when you least expect it. It's not every day you have your parents break the news to you that your best friend has committed suicide. It's one of those days where I just have that gut feeling that something is bound to go wrong—and trust me, I've had more than one of those days—but never in my life could I have imagined something going this wrong.

The memory of hearing of my best friend's death is as fresh in my mind as ink on a sheet of paper. The days after hearing of her death are a blur of tears and locking myself in my room all day, convincing myself that this is all just some cruel joke. I soon learned this to be the first stage of grieving—denial. I'm not ready to move on, but I know I have to try because even if she isn't here to live her life with me, I know that she will want me to live mine for the both of us. Even if I'm still angry and confused about why hers ended.

* * *

I sit in my car and stare up at my high school. The lawn is littered with teens conversing about what they did over break, going on as if absolutely nothing has changed when it feels like my whole world has changed. Taking a deep breath, I grab my things before opening the car door and stepping out. Putting my head down, I try to walk briskly into the building without having to run into anyone.

"Alexa!" *Just my luck.*

"Paige, hi." I force some enthusiasm into my voice, but it just ends up falling flat. "I heard what happened, and the girls and I just wanted to say sorry for your loss. If you ever need anything, I will be happy to help," she says with what I can obviously tell is fake sincerity. I look at her and the rest of the girls sitting at a table a few feet away.

"Thanks for your concern, Paige," I say, forcing down any hint of anger. "But I'm fine." I abruptly turn around and walk away before she can get a chance to reply.

Walking through the crowded hallway, I glance at the place where my best friend's locker used to be. The place where I would meet with her every day to complain about how awful our mornings were as we headed to our first class together. The place I will no longer be going to every morning. I trudge through the halls with memories surging my mind as I try hard not to break down right here and now. It's hard enough waking up this morning and driving past her house on my way here, but this . . . this just adds salt to the wound. The shrill ringing of the bell breaks me out of my trance, and I hurry to my locker before heading off to my first class of the day.

I can't seem to focus as Ms. Anderson promptly starts the lesson. I can't stop hearing her voice at the back of my head or picturing her next to me, not paying attention to the lesson at all as she makes snarky comments about how awful Ms. Anderson's outfit choice is that day.

"Alexa? Ms. Parker, are you with us?" The sound of Ms. Anderson's saccharine voice interrupts any further thoughts, and I try to clear my head.

"Yes. Sorry," I say quickly. She gives me a sympathetic look before continuing with the lesson, a lump forming in my throat. Time seems to be moving agonizingly slow as my next few classes go by; it doesn't help that every few minutes, I am approached by people saying how sorry they are for my loss and how she was such an amazing person. Half of them don't even know her. It infuriates me that these people didn't give her a second thought when she was alive, but now that she's dead, she suddenly matters to them.

When lunch finally comes around, I sit at a table towards the back. I'm relieved to get a break and a chance to sort my thoughts. My break is short-lived as I'm joined by company.

"Hi, Alexa. How are you?" Alison greets timidly as she and Madison sit down with their lunch trays. Alison and Madison are twins and probably the sweetest girls you will ever meet, but right now, I just wish they will get up and leave. I'm tired of people coming up to me with their pity and condolences, which only reminds me more of my loss.

"I'm fine," I reply half-heartedly, not having it in me to ask them to leave. "What brings you guys here?"

"Can't we have lunch with our captain?" Madison says with that bright smile that can light up any room.

"We just want to check on you, and the team wants to know if you'll be at cheer practice today." *Right. There's practice.*

"Yeah, totally." I flash them a smile. I can't let them see my weakness, and if moving on means that I have to resume the role of the girl I was before that day, then so be it. As lunch progresses and they make no move to leave, I struggle to stay focused. Everything reminds me of her.

The table near the center of the room used to be our table. The table we would sit at every day and talk about boys while also discussing our future. She would always talk about how we would attend the same college and become roommates and then rent an apartment together in a different city after graduation. It all just keeps leading me back to the question of 'why?'. I can feel my eyes start to blur with tears, and I stand up suddenly. The twins look up at me with concern-filled eyes.

"I-I'm going to go. I just remembered I have to go to the library and check out a book for my next class," I say while grabbing my things.

"Oh okay. I guess we'll see you at practice?" Alison asks.

"I'll be there," I promise her.

I emerge from the cafeteria and make my way to the bathroom with my eyes locked on the ground so no one can see the tears ready to fall.

"Sorry," I say after accidentally bumping into someone, not even bothering to look at them as I start to sprint to the bathroom in my frantic state. After making sure it's empty, I slide against the wall and do the one thing I promised myself I wouldn't do today—I cry. The tears pour out like a waterfall, the confusion and anger and pain with them. I cry until my vision is blurry and my eyes are red. I cry until I know that I can't be in here any longer because someone is bound to walk in, and I'm not sure I can handle confrontation in this state. It's been a month since she's been gone, and instead of things getting easier with time, everything seems to be getting harder. I wish that I can just go back in time and stop any of this from happening.

It's taking me some time to compose myself. I missed the remainder of my classes for the day, and I can't even bring myself to care. I end up leaving cheer practice early at the suggestion of the team. I can't focus on the routine, and I was messing everything up. Pushing through the double doors of the gym, I let out a frustrated sigh as I lean against the wall and pinch the bridge of my nose. I eventually head to the school's parking lot, which is mostly empty with the exception of a few cars.

"Alexa?" I hear my name being called and I go rigid. *Why can't I be left alone?*

"Hey, Matt." I turn to look at him and his friends surrounding his truck with sweat and dirt running down their faces. Matt Carpenter is the quarterback of our school's football team. I don't really recall having any real interactions with him other than at football games.

"It's been awhile since I've seen you," he says.

"I have a lot going on at the moment." I unlock my car door, not caring to continue this conversation after the crap day I've had.

"Wait," he says as I'm about to make my escape. I look at him expectantly, feeling annoyed that I'm being delayed from leaving.

"I'm sorry but I need to go." I shut my car door and leave, not allowing myself to feel bad for how harsh that probably sounded. When I finally enter my house, I'm greeted by the smell of my mother's cooking.

Before, I would be rushing into the kitchen, anxious to get a bite of whatever was on the stove. Now, I barely have an appetite.

"How was school?" she inquires with a smile as I throw my keys down on to the table.

"It was okay." Sighing, I watch as she dumps some pasta into the pot of boiling water.

"You know you can talk to me, Alexa. What happened isn't something you can easily recover from," she starts with a soft gaze in her eyes as she looks at me. "I know you both were close but—" I clench my hands into fists at her words.

We weren't *just* close; she was all I had. She's the only person that understood me, and now, she's gone. No explanation, no warning, and no apology.

"Mom, I know you're trying to help me and I appreciate it; I really do, but I just need time and space. She's my best friend and I don't want to think about the fact that she's gone." She looks taken aback by my words but she nods anyway.

"Okay. Well, I'm here if you need anything. I just want you to know that you're not alone," she replies with a sad smile, and I give her a quick hug before heading upstairs to my room. I lock the door and collapse on to my bed as I stare up at the ceiling. I grab my journal from the nightstand and open it up to a clean page but I freeze as a picture falls out.

It's of her and I at a party. We were holding red solo cups—which were filled with ginger ale—and smiling like there was no tomorrow.

"I can't believe you did that!" I exclaim as we both stumble into my room, hunched over in fits of laughter. *"The look on her face was priceless!"*

"It was definitely an accident," Cam says with a smirk.

"I think Paige knows you spilling that drink on her wasn't an accident."

I shut the journal and hold it tightly to my chest. It isn't fair. It isn't fair that Cam is gone, and I'm expected to just move on. How can I when most of my happiest memories are with her? How can I when all I can think about is her day in and day out? The tears fall down my cheeks for what feels like the thousandth time today. I curl into a ball with the picture clenched against my chest. I don't know how long I stayed like that, but before I know it, I'm asleep.

CHAPTER TWO

It's been two months since her death, and I can feel myself drifting away from reality with each passing day. I feel numb. I felt so much during these past few weeks that, now, I feel nothing. Some might say that I was depressed, which is the fourth stage of grieving according to the school's counselor.

"Are you sure you want to do this?" she asks. I nod as I slump further into the chair.

"Alexa, you do realize that by you dropping all of these extracurricular activities—"

"Yes, I know," I interject, looking at my counselor. "But I just don't have the time to manage all of these clubs, and everything is just too difficult for me at the moment . . ." I trail off. The brief look of pity that passes over her face tells me that she knows what, or more like whom, I'm referring to.

"So you're sure you want to—"

"Positive," I affirm, willing her to stop fighting me on this.

"Okay then. As you wish." Ms. Vega sighs in defeat as I get up and make my way out of her office.

The hallways are crowded when I exit the office doors and head in the direction of the cafeteria. There's one more thing I need to do, and I have to do it before I convince myself otherwise. I saunter up to the table where the cheer team sits with a newfound determination in my stride. I can feel everyone's eyes on me—

watching, calculating, waiting to see the scene that is about to unfold.

"I quit." As soon as the words leave my mouth, they all look up at me with dumbfounded expressions.

"What?" Mackenzie, who is our flyer, questions, not quite understanding what I'm trying to say.

"I quit the team. I resign from my position as captain." Their faces go from confusion to shock, and Alison immediately stands up as if to protest.

"What do you mean you quit? Alexa, don't do this," she says sternly.

"I'm sorry," I reply. "But this isn't me anymore."

I turn to Paige who's trying not to show how happy she is at the turn of events. Now that I have given up my position as captain, it will now be passed down to her after all.

"Congrats, Paige. Finally got what you've always wanted." I turn away from the table and amble out of the cafeteria, trying to hold my head up high.

Not only did I just give away my position, I gave away my status too.

I make my way through the empty hallways and into the school's library, the only place where I know I can be alone.

That's when it all hits me.

* * *

Do I really want to do this? Give up everything I've worked for since freshman year just like that? I decided that yes, I'm done being that girl.

I'm done being the stereotypical high school cheerleader who has the whole school wrapped around her fingers. I'm done putting everyone else's best interests before mine, and I'm definitely done trying to be someone I'm not. All these years, I've been everyone else's image of what a perfect teenage girl should be and look like, but I am far from perfect; I'm not anything like that girl I pretended to be. I'm finally done, and the worst part is that it took my best friend dying for me to realize that I had it all wrong—that none of this high school crap matters.

I pull my hair into a ponytail as I look around the library and remember that I need to check out *The Scarlet Letter* for my literature class. I rummage through every related category I can think of but with no luck. I collapse into a chair, growing frustrated. I get up to leave the library before my eyes land on a small shelf across the room labeled 'Classics'. *How did I not see that?* I sigh in relief and rush to grab the book off the shelf before heading towards the librarian to check it out.

"I'd like to check this book out." I give her my best smile and hand her the book.

"Student ID," she says. I hold my ID out so she can scan it.

"Sorry, hun. Says here you have an obligation for an overdue book. I can't let you check out any more books until you return it." It takes me a moment to register the book she's talking about, but then I remember that I checked that book out last year for a project and have probably misplaced it by now.

"I really need this book for my English class. I promise I'll return it," I plead.

"Sorry, hun." She shrugs. "Rules are rules."

I groan internally as my eyes wander around the library, as if some answer to my problem will magically appear. Just as I'm about to try making a run for it with the book in hand, the door opens and someone walks in carrying a stack of boxes.

"Miss Everly," he greets. I manage to get a peek at his black hair and green eyes. "I have those copies you wanted."

"How kind of you, Blake." She smiles cheerily at him. "Just set them there." She turns back to me as if just noticing that I am still standing here. "Like I said, Miss Parker, there's nothing I can do."

I nod, knowing this entire situation isn't her fault. I thank the elderly librarian before making my way out of the library. I guess I can just go to the public library or order my own copy.

I open my locker, gathering my books for my next couple of classes before slamming it shut and jumping a bit when I see the same guy from the library standing beside me.

"Hey." His voice resounds through the empty hallway that will be swarmed with noisy teens in a few minutes. "It seemed like you really needed this."

I look down to see him extending the copy of *The Scarlet Letter*. I tentatively take it from him; I was both surprised and confused.

"Thank you." I sigh in relief. "Blake, right?"

"Yeah." He nods, his mouth quirking into a smile. "I never got your name."

"Alexa." I offer my hand. He grips it firmly, giving it a light shake. "Parker."

"Harper," he replies. "Blake Harper."

CHAPTER THREE

When Mrs. Smith, my best friend's mom, shows up at our doorstep with a flustered look on her face and envelope in hand, I am completely taken by surprise. I haven't seen or spoken to her since the funeral and didn't expect to after that considering that I am her dead daughter's best friend. So if she's here, it must be important.

"Mrs. Smith, how are you? Would you like to come in?" I ask uneasily after a few long seconds of me just staring at her in shock. Her hair is slightly disheveled, and her eyes are a little bloodshot as if she cried before coming here.

"No thanks, dear," she responds, politely declining my invitation. "I just want to give you this." She extends the envelope to me, and my hand starts to shake as I recognize the loopy handwriting that belongs to my best friend.

"What is it?" I question, my voice wavering.

"A letter, I believe. We found it in her room while going through some stuff. Had your name on it so I thought you should have it." She lets out a sigh, and that's when I notice how completely drained she looks, as if all the life has been sucked out of her. I guess, in a way, it has.

"I should get going now. Take care, Alexa." She forces a small smile on her face as she walks down the driveway and to her car. When I'm sure she's gone, I shut the door and quickly run upstairs with the envelope pressed to my chest.

Here I am, moments later, sitting down in the middle of my room with tears in my eyes as I look down at the envelope addressed to me with no idea of what the hell to do. This is from her, and it's addressed to me and I can't quite process it. Am I curious about the contents of this envelope? Yes, very much so. Do I really want to know this very moment what it contains? I don't know. That's the problem. I don't know much of anything anymore. This envelope can hold the answers I'm looking for as to why she did it, but as I continue to stare at the envelope, it starts to feel heavy in my hands; I can't bring myself to open it—at least not yet anyway.

I like to think that part of the reason why is because I'm just not ready, but I know what's really keeping me from reading the contents of that envelope—it's the fear of what I will find. As I wipe my eyes and put the envelope in a place where only I will be able to find it, I can't help but think that maybe, just maybe, all of this is my fault.

* * *

After an uneventful weekend, which I mostly spent worrying, it's time to go back to school. I shower, get dressed, feign a smile, and kiss my parents goodbye as I head out the door.

It's the same routine every day. The only difference today is, instead of going to my third-hour home economics class, I go to poetry due to a schedule change. The desks in the classroom are set up in groups of four, and I immediately gravitate towards the back.

"Alexa, thank God you're in this class," a familiar voice says with relief. I turn and I'm met with the identical green eyes of Alison and Madison.

"I didn't know you guys were into poetry," I say questioningly as I take a seat in the desk adjacent to theirs.

"We don't," they say in unison. "Our dad made us sign up for it. He says we need to have more appreciation for the finer arts, whatever that means," Alison finishes while rolling her eyes.

I almost laugh at her obvious distaste for this class, but that urge to laugh suddenly disappears as Blake Harper waltzes into the classroom. Alison and Madison notice my mood change, and they both roll their eyes when they see what I'm looking at, or more specifically, who I'm looking at.

"Hey, little sis. Other little sis," Blake says with a smirk as he pats them on their heads.

"Sis?" I ask, my brows furrowing in confusion. That's when I notice it; they all have the same green eyes and shiny black hair.

"Alexa, this thing right here . . ." Madison pauses as she looks at Blake as if he's the worst thing she has ever laid eyes on. "Is our brother." No matter how disgusted she tries to look, I can see the smile in her eyes.

"We're triplets. Unfortunately," Alison states and my eyes widen in shock.

"Triplets?" I exclaim.

It puzzles me how I have never noticed him before, considering that I've cheered with the girls since freshman year, but then again, I never paid much attention to anything other than myself before everything happened. Maybe if I had just paid more attention, things won't be the way they are now.

"I see why you wouldn't be able to tell considering we're the better looking ones," Alison jokes.

"That cut me deep, little sis." Blake feigns hurt as he presses his hand on his heart.

"Stop calling me little sis! You're only older by two minutes."

"Best two minutes of my life."

Before they can continue their banter, a petite woman with blonde hair walks in and tells everyone to be seated. Blake takes the remaining seat in our group next to me, and I try not to think about how close he is to me and how I can feel the warmth emanating from his body.

"I guess we'll be seeing more of each other," Blake whispers. I can feel my face heating up as I turn away from him and try to focus on the lesson.

CHAPTER FOUR

I enter my therapists' office after school despite my insistence to my mother that there is no reason for me to go anymore, and that sending me to these sessions is pointless and a waste of money. If there is one thing you should know about my mother, it's that she's stubborn. It's that stubbornness that gets her anything she wants; hence, me attending this session.

"Katherine," I acknowledge the middle-aged woman as I plop down on the love seat in the middle of the room.

"Alexa, welcome back!" Katherine's voice is saccharine as she smiles while pulling out her clipboard.

"So how are you?" she asks me. That is always the first thing she asks during our sessions, and she always receives the same answer.

"I'm fine." I try to stay as guarded as possible. I hate coming to these sessions, much less like the idea of someone trying to pick away at my emotions and determine how I feel when I don't even know how I feel myself. We sit in silence for a few seconds, and I look around the room, trying to focus on anything but her.

"Alexa, sometimes you can hurt yourself more than anyone else can just by keeping everything bottled up. So tell me, how are you really?" She speaks to me in the way a mother would speak to a toddler while trying not to upset them.

"As I said before, I'm fine." I rest my head on my hand and watch her scribble something down on her clipboard.

"Can you tell me about Cam?" My body goes rigid at the mention of her name. She notices and I make an effort to regain my composure.

"What do you want to know?" I reply coldly.

"Tell me what she was like; what your relationship with her was like."

"She was my best friend. There's no amount of words I could use to make you understand." I look down at my hands as I clasp them together.

I don't want to tell Katherine anything. I don't trust myself to talk about Cam without crying, and that's something I'm not willing to do. Especially not in front of some woman who thinks she can get me to open up to her when I can't even open up to my own parents.

After what feels like an eternity of endless questions I don't want to answer, the session is finally over. Upon arriving home, I greet my parents and go straight to my room, deciding to skip dinner.

Today's session stressed me out, and I feel like screaming and crying and throwing something. Instead, I finish my homework and go straight to bed.

* * *

I put my keys down on the table as I enter the kitchen with my phone in hand and my brows furrowed in confusion. She wasn't at school today and she hasn't been answering the thousands of text messages I've been sending her all day asking her if she's okay. Sighing, I make my way upstairs and into my bedroom. I decide to call her one more time, but she doesn't pick up, to my chagrin.

What is going on? I think to myself as millions of horrible thoughts enter my mind. She has been acting weird lately, and when I asked her about it, she said it was just the stress of getting ready to get back to school. A horrible feeling settles in the pit of my stomach. I rush downstairs and into the kitchen, grabbing my keys.

"*Alexa?" My mom enters from the family room as I'm about to head out the door with a weird look on her face.*

"*Hey, Mom. I was just heading out."*

"*Alexa, I need to tell you something." She has this sad look in her eyes, and I know this is serious. The last time I saw my mom like this was when she found out that her grandmother, my great-grandma, passed away.*

"*Mom, what's wrong?" I urge.*

"*Alexa, I don't know how to say this to you, but Cameron, s-she committed suicide." At that moment, it felt like the world stopped. My keys dropped out of my hand and on to the floor as I sank to my knees. It all felt like some sort of dream.*

"*No," I say slowly. "You're lying." My body suddenly feels heavy, like I can't support my own weight. I look at my mother, urging her with my eyes to tell me that this isn't true—that I misheard her—but she looks at me with a look of pity with tears brimming her eyes as she shakes her head at me, confirming that it isn't a lie.*

"*No," I say. "No, no, no!" I can feel the tears pouring down my cheeks. I knew something was wrong. I knew I should have gone to check on her as soon as she didn't show up to school because she never misses a day of school. I knew something was wrong the moment she started acting weird. Sobs rack through my body as my mother pulls me into a hug.*

"*I'm so sorry," she whispers. "So, so sorry." I can feel my mother's body shaking as she, too, shed her own tears. She loves Cam as if she were her own.*

"*I should've done something. It's all my fault!" I scream over and over and over until, finally, it all stops.*

I bolt awake, panting heavily. My hair is plastered on to my forehead with sweat. My heart is pounding in my chest, and a feeling of dread settles over me. It's just a nightmare; the same one that plays on a constant loop every night like a broken record with no hope of ever getting it to stop.

CHAPTER FIVE

After sitting through a few classes and being scolded in each one for not focusing, I finally find myself sitting at a lunch table and staring down at my tray of Tater tots.

"I can't believe you just did that." I hold my stomach as I double over in laughter.

"What? She was being rude," Cam replies innocently. If you know Cam as well as I do, you will know that smug smile on her face is anything but innocent.

"You threw a Tater tot at her, Cam!" I laugh even more as she pops one in her mouth. We sit there, laughing together. To me, it was just a regular day. Who knew that moments like those could be cut short?

"Hey, Alexa!" Alison beams as she and Madison take a seat at the table. They seem to be making an appearance in my life more often now.

"Hi." I flash a smile that doesn't meet my eyes. "How are you guys? How's the team?"

"Oh, we quit," Madison says nonchalantly as if it were something completely unimportant, and she rolls her eyes at the look on my face.

"Look, ever since you quit and Paige took over as captain, she's been parading us around as if we are nothing but mere peasants who are only there for her to bark orders at. You can't even call it a team anymore."

I can't help but feel like this is my fault. I was the glue that held everything together, and now that I can't even hold myself together, everything is falling apart.

"Alexa, it's not your fault so get that look off your face," Alison scolds me. "We understand why you had to quit."

It doesn't feel right that they're quitting the team so easily because of me, and I can't quite understand why they're making an effort to suddenly be my friends. I don't need their pity, and I definitely don't want to be anyone's charity case. After lunch, I decide to go to the library knowing that it will be near-empty and also hoping to start reading *The Scarlet Letter* so that Mr. Callaghan will stop threatening to call my parents about me being behind. I navigate to the back of the library, pulling down the sleeves of my sweatshirt. It's very cold here, and I regret not carrying a warmer jacket with me today.

"You know . . ." a voice starts and I jump a little, startled, as I turn to meet the depthless eyes of Blake Harper. They're a greenish-blue color today. Almost like the ocean.

"It's starting to feel like wherever I go, there you are. Is there something you want to confess?" he finishes with that awful smirk of his.

"Excuse me? You think I'm stalking you or something?" I snort at the thought.

"Your words, not mine." He shrugs as he makes his way past me to put a book back on the shelf. I roll my eyes and walk away, settling into a secluded area in the corner of the library where I won't be bothered.

Upon arriving home later that day, I head straight to my room and immediately get started on homework. My grades aren't as good as they used to be, and I definitely don't want to fail my senior year. I'm nearly done when my mom calls me down for dinner.

"Hey." I sit down at the table and quickly notice the absence of my father. "Where's Dad?"

"At work," she answers while forking some parmesan chicken into her mouth. "He's working on a new case and it's a big one."

My father is always working late these days, and it bothers me.

"How was school?" she inquires.

Horrible. It has been every day since Cam's been gone.

"Good," I say.

I make a show of stuffing food into my mouth to avoid her gaze. *Please let it go,* I plead in my head because that look on my mother's face tells me that she knows I'm lying and that she wants to press the topic even further.

"How's cheerleading?" she asks.

"It's going great. The girls are excited about championships." I don't know why I lied and why I don't tell her that I quit the team. *It shouldn't be that big a deal, right?*

"Alexa," she starts as she puts her fork down and looks at me. "Ms. Vega called and told me that you dropped all of your extracurricular activities, including student council, then she goes on to tell me how she's heard news about you quitting the cheer team." She looks at me with that stern look on her face that makes me want to slump down on to my chair.

"Okay, fine. It's true," I rush out. Lying to my mother is bad enough but getting caught is even worse.

"I don't understand why you're suddenly deciding to just drop all your activities. Is this about Cam—"

I cut her off before she can finish the sentence.

"No, this isn't about Cam," I say, trying to convince her, but it sounds more like I'm trying to convince myself. "I'm not hungry anymore." I push my plate away, suddenly at a loss for appetite.

"Alexa, just sit down and talk to me. I want to help you," she pleads and the look in her eyes breaks my heart.

"Mom, I'm just really tired and need to get some sleep. Can we please do this another time?" I feel bad for leaving her clueless and without an explanation as to what's going on with me.

But how can I explain it to her when I can't even explain it to myself?

CHAPTER SIX

I feel it all at once—the sadness and grief and confusion. It all comes rushing in the second I wake up with tears rolling down my cheeks as my heart beats faster and faster and faster. Today is November fourth, Cam's birthday. It's her eighteenth birthday and she isn't even here to celebrate it. She isn't here to be jolted awake as I burst into her bedroom too early in the morning and wish her a happy birthday. She isn't here for me to see her face light up with happiness as she opens the gift I will have spent hours at the mall looking for, just to make sure it was perfect. She isn't here. Realizing that, as I do every morning, hurts; it hurts like hell.

"Alexa? It's time to get up or you'll be late for school." I start to wipe the tears rolling down my cheeks at the sound of my mother's voice on the other side of the door. The last thing I need is for her to come in and see me crying.

"Alexa?" She knocks on the door as she calls my name again. I want to tell her that I'm not feeling well, that I can't go to school today, but then I think of Cam again. I think about how if she were here, she would tell me that locking myself in my room and crying all day isn't going to get me anywhere. That doing whatever this is, isn't going to bring her back. She's gone; she's really gone. I can feel my eyes start to water all over again at the realization. All I've been doing these past couple of weeks is cry. I'm haunted by the memories of someone I wish I can forget but can't let go of. I wish I can just erase her from my mind because maybe then, I won't feel so guilty.

"Alexa, are you up?" My doorknob starts to jiggle.

"I'll be down in a few minutes," I say, trying to sound like I'm not crying. Only when I can hear the sound of my mom's retreating footsteps do I slowly get out of bed.

I'm going to try to make this day special for Cam. I manage to put together a decent outfit and throw my hair up into a ponytail as I grab my bag, deciding that it isn't worth the effort of putting layers of concealer on my face.

"Morning!" my mom chirps as she pours some coffee into my dad's cup. I nod at them both as I grab an apple and make my way out the door, knowing that if I don't leave now, I will surely be late for school.

"Happy birthday, Cam," I whisper before pulling out of my driveway and trying to swallow the lump in my throat.

Upon arrival, I head straight to my locker while keeping my head down as I try to ignore the stares of people most likely wondering what I'm becoming—what I'm allowing myself to become. I grab my books and take a deep breath before closing my locker. I glance at Cam's locker, which is just down the hall. My blood runs cold at the sight of the decorative banner hanging above it.

Happy Birthday, Cameron! R.I.P.

I can feel my face begin to heat up in anger as I stare at Paige and watch as she proudly stands in front of the banner with a small crowd of people around her. My self-control deceives me, and before I know it, I'm marching towards her and angrily tearing down the banner, earning shocked gasps as the crowd grows bigger.

"Alexa! What are you—" Paige shrieks.

"Save it," I cut her off, striking my hand against her cheek as adrenaline courses through me. "Who are you trying to fool, Paige?" She scowls at me.

"I'm just trying to show some appreciation for our beloved friend." She holds her now red cheek as she glares daggers at me.

"Beloved friend?" I scoff. "She wasn't your beloved friend when you spread rumors about her to the entire school!" I scream, causing Paige to flinch. I can feel my voice start to wobble as I glare at her. She starts looking around at the crowd that's gathered as her face tinged with embarrassment.

"And she definitely wasn't your beloved friend when she killed herself, and you didn't even care enough to attend her damn funeral!" By now, I'm yelling loud enough for even the people at the end of the hallway to hear.

"You have the audacity to call yourself her friend after trying to make her life hell here?" I say at a much lower volume before throwing the crumpled banner in my hands on to the floor. I pay no attention to everyone's eyes on me as I run to the closest bathroom and enter the last stall. I slide against the wall and burst into tears.

I'm so sorry, Cam.

I begin to sob uncontrollably, and it feels like the weight of the world is crashing down on to my chest. I need to get out of here; I have to get out of here.

I pick up my bag and rush out of the stall, feeling the sudden urge to be anywhere but here. Putting my hand over my mouth to quiet my sobs, I rush through the hallways and out through the front doors of the school.

"Alexa?" Someone's calling my name, and I ignore them as I keep walking.

"Alexa, wait." The person grabs my hand and I turn around, not bothering to hide my tears.

"What do you want, Blake?" I spit out, yanking my hand away.

"What's wrong? Do you need me to get my sisters?" he asks frantically with concern filling his eyes. For some reason, I just want him to comfort me, to let me know that everything is going to be okay, but nothing will ever be okay anymore.

Not when Cam's gone, leaving me to slowly pick up the shattered pieces of my life.

"Just leave me alone." I turn on my heels and leave Blake there; he's probably wondering what the hell is wrong with me. Does he even know about Cam and what happened to her? Did he see everything that happened in that hallway moments ago?

My hands are shaking as I make way down road after road, not really sure where I'm going. I can't bring myself to care as the tears continue to stream down my face like a dam that's lost all stability. And then there it is. The large engraved headstone that stands above my best friend who is buried six feet under. I haven't been here since her funeral, and that's mostly because I can't bring myself to come. I get out of the car and just stand there; I stand there alone and broken. Broken because of the girl who chose to leave too soon. Broken because of the girl who was supposed to someday be my maid of honor. Broken because of the girl who was supposed to stick around forever.

I kneel down, instantly overwhelmed by the proximity between me and her grave. I can't handle being here. I can't handle being in the spot where my best friend is now lying dead and decaying. I will never recover from this, but there's one thing that might ease the aching pain in my chest, and that's to say the words I never got the chance to.

"Hey, Cam," I speak as if she's sitting right next to me, and maybe she is. Maybe she's silently watching me as I slowly break down right in front of her grave. "First of all, happy birthday," I continue, my voice wavering. "I miss you." I choke as my vision begins to blur with more tears. I manage to compose myself and continue to speak.

"Things aren't the same without you," I say. "And I'm sorry. I'm sorry that I didn't notice you needed help. I'm sorry that

I couldn't stop you that day." I can't hold it all in any longer. It feels like my heart has been torn out of my chest.

"Please come back. I can't live like this."

After a few minutes of just sitting there and crying, I look up at the sky, which is starting to become gray and cloudy with the promise of rain. I wipe my swollen eyes, standing up from my spot on the ground. I gaze at the bouquet of roses that someone must have put there recently. Roses were her favorite. I run my fingers gently over her headstone and whisper my final words.

"I love you."

CHAPTER SEVEN

I hide my head under my hoodie as I step foot in to my high school. I won't even be here now if it were up to me, but my mother was furious at me when I came home last night. She demanded why I wasn't at school, why I was doing this to myself, why I was ruining my life.

I turn and see Alison, Madison, and Blake emerge from around a corner. My eyes lock with Blake's momentarily before I quickly avert my gaze. Not bothering to stop for them, I turn and keep on walking. I don't deserve friends like them, and they don't deserve to put up with the hot mess my life has become. Maybe it's meant to be like this. Maybe I don't deserve friends; I couldn't even keep my only true friend from killing herself.

"Alexa!" the girls call. I keep on walking, hoping that they will just get the hint and leave me alone.

"Alexa, wait!" I stop as someone grabs my shoulder and I reluctantly turn around.

"Hey, you didn't hear us calling you back there?" Alison questions with an oblivious smile while Madison and Blake are behind her. When I don't answer and look anywhere but them, they begin to take in my appearance with concern flooding their eyes.

"We didn't see you at all yesterday," Madison says. "Are you okay?"

"I'm fine. Just wasn't feeling it yesterday." I begin to wonder if they heard about what went down yesterday, if they heard about the crap Paige tried to pull, and if Blake told them of our encounter as I fled from school.

The warning bell rings, signaling that class is about to start soon. Madison smacks her hand over her head as she groans.

"Crap. Alison, we have to hurry up and turn some late work in before class starts." She turns to me and engulfs me in a hug before pulling away and resting her hands on my shoulders.

"Let us know if you need anything, okay?"

I head towards my locker as they walk away, but Blake swiftly grabs my arm. "Why are you doing this?" he asks frustratedly. "Why can't you just let them be your friends?"

His question catches me off guard but my shock quickly disappears as my face hardens.

"Let go of me, Blake."

"Why are you pushing them away when they're clearly trying to help you?" He doesn't let go but his grip on my arm loosens. I remain quiet as my mind searches for an answer to his question. He's right; I do push them away. I push them away because the one time I had someone I could count on, she left; she killed herself.

"Because people always leave," I finally say as I rip my arm away and shove past him, leaving him standing in the middle of the hallway. He watches as I storm off.

I sit in class an hour later, desperately staring at the clock as I wait for this class to end.

"Miss Parker, may I have a word with you?" Mrs. Anderson questions, keeping me from bolting out of the room as soon as the bell rings. Mrs. Anderson signals me to take a seat in front of her desk, and I huff before slumping into the chair.

"What's the problem?" I mumble, pulling down the sleeves of my hoodie over my hands.

"Is everything okay?" And there it is; the question everyone asks as if they don't already know about what happened, as if Cam and her death haven't been the talk of the school for the past few weeks now. I'm getting tired of hearing the same question over and over, and it's starting to drive me crazy. Maybe that's what's happening to me; maybe I am going crazy.

"You seriously haven't heard?" I ask, annoyance evident in my tone. "You haven't heard about how my best friend committed suicide?" She doesn't bother to reprimand me for my tone as she nods.

"Miss Parker, I'm sorry for your loss, I really am and I know it's tough, but you can't let that define you. Your grades are goin—"

"To shape my future, I know," I cut her off. "But no one seems to understand that I just lost the one person in my life who I could truly depend on, and you may not have cared about her but I did." I shake my head and stand up, abruptly leaving the room. I exit the school, deciding to go to the pier across the street to clear my mind. I gaze over the water, admiring the waves and the warm breeze that came with them. I admire how serene everything is compared to how tumultuous my life feels.

I'm heartbroken and angry and sad. I feel hurt physically and emotionally. All these days I've spent wondering what I could've done to stop her, and how I didn't notice she was screaming for help. I hate myself for everything that's happened. I just wish I could see her. I wish I could hug her and apologize for being a horrible friend. A tear slips from my eye along with an idea. I could be with her if I just did the same thing. I have nothing to live for anymore. My grades are horrific, my family won't even notice, and I don't have any friends to care. I stare down at the water, realizing how high up I am. One jump and it will all end. The pain, the suffering—it will all be over.

I look around, not wanting anyone to stop me from what I'm about to do. I climb over the railing and stand at the edge of the pier. My breathing is heavy, and I can't stop the tears gliding down my cheeks. I begin to breathe harder and harder as I stare down at the beautiful blue water. It's as if it's beckoning for me to jump in, promising me that if I do, I'll receive the peace that I crave, so I do; I jump into the water and feel the coldness of it the moment I submerge. Everything is quiet. The noise of the world is drowned out, and it's almost peaceful. I close my eyes, letting myself sink deeper and deeper. This is it. This is the end and I'm ready for it. No more pain. No more suffering.

Suddenly, my eyes snap open as water starts to enter through my nose and into my lungs. My body begins to inhale the water, and my mind begins to panic. It feels like I'm being suffocated, but this is what I want, right? To just end it all? A burning sensation begins to take place in my lungs as my body starts to take in more water, desperately needing oxygen. I try to move my arms, but I just sink deeper. I just want this to be over. *When will it be over?* My vision starts to get blurry, and I can hear my heart beating slower and slower. The edges of my vision start to get dark, and I know I'm losing consciousness. *This is it*, I think as I fall into oblivion.

CHAPTER EIGHT

All I see is darkness. The repetitive beeps are sounding from every angle, and suddenly, my eyes shoot open. A stinging sensation pierces through my eyes as the room's light hits me. Once my eyes adjust to the brightness, my head begins to pound as if it has been smashed against pavement.

I try moving but my body is stiff. My eyes trail down my body, confused at all the wires and tubes connected in scattered areas throughout the upper half of my body and arms. I try searching my mind for any memory of anything but I fail. A knock on the door snaps me out of my trance. I turn my head towards the entrance to see a nurse walk in, pushing a cart in front of her. I furrow my eyebrows, still not comprehending the situation or why I'm here in the first place. My throat feels as dry as a desert. I attempt to reach for the water on my bedside, only to fail miserably and knock it on to the floor. The nurse notices that I'm awake and quickly refills the cup, bringing it up to my mouth. I drink until the cup is empty.

"Why am I here?" I manage to ask. She gives me a sad smile.

"I'll call your parents here and let them explain. They've been waiting for two days." Using all my strength, I try sitting up but barely make it an inch off the bed. The door bursts open, and my mother's weary body rushes to my side.

"Oh thank god!" she cries, engulfing me into her arms.

"You're okay!" My dad sighs in relief as he kisses my wrapped forehead.

"Mom," I croak. Her eyes look up to me in response.

"Why am I here?" She looks at my father who nods. She takes a deep breath before tightening her grip on my hand.

"You jumped off the pier," she replies shakily. "Why would you do something like that?" My heart aches at the sight of tears rolling down her cheeks. At that moment, everything becomes clear. Memories begin to flood my mind. Images of the water and the pitch black darkness flash before me. Everything after that is a blur.

"How did you find me?" I whisper, my body feeling numb. I start to wonder if any of this is real—if I'm dreaming.

"Someone saw you at the pier and immediately called 911," she says, her voice wavering at every word.

"But who call—" I burst into a coughing fit, and I'm pushed back down on to the bed when I try to get up.

"I will explain everything later. Just relax." She envelopes me into a hug and squeezes me tight like she has no intention of letting go. I don't realize I'm crying until a sob escapes my mouth.

"I'm so sorry," I whisper. We stay like that for a while; I'm wrapped in my mother's arms and my dad being a comforting presence to the both of us.

I wake up what seems to be a couple of hours later. My mother is asleep in the chair next to my bed, and my dad is nowhere to be seen. There's a knock at the door, and Alison and Madison walk in with the person I least expect, Blake. I take a sharp intake of breath as his eyes stare into mine, an unreadable expression on his face. *Why are they here?* I didn't want them here especially in the state I'm in and under the circumstances that got me here.

"I'm sorry, I must have fallen asleep. You're Alexa's friends? The ones I spoke to earlier?" My mother stands up, stirred awake from her sleep.

"Yes. It's nice to meet you in person. I'm Alison, and this is my sister Madison, and my brother Blake." As if on cue, my dad walks in with two cups of coffee.

"Honey, these are Alexa's friends," my mom explains and he nods in acknowledgment as he hands my mother a cup of coffee.

"Mom," I finally speak. "Do you think you can get me some soup?"

"Are you sure you don't want anything else? You haven't eaten in two days," my mom questions, coming over to smooth the hair out of my face. I can't even imagine how I must look right now.

"I really don't think I can stomach anything else." Since I woke up, I've been suppressing the urge to throw up.

"Okay." She nods, looking towards the girls and Blake. "Do you guys want anything?"

"No thanks, Mrs. Parker," they reply in unison. When both of my parents exit the room, they immediately make their way to my bedside.

"How are you feeling?" Alison asks me as she sits beside the bed. Blake stands against the far wall while Madison takes the spot next to Alison. Their eyes look puffy and red as if they've been crying all day.

"Like crap." I try to lighten the mood, but they don't even crack a smile as their brows furrow in concern.

"Alexa, why?" I don't even need to ask what they're talking about.

"I don't wanna talk about it," I say, shifting in my hospital gown.

"You're going to have to talk to someone about this at some point," Madison says.

I nod, knowing that I'm going straight to a psychologist after I leave this hospital. Not because it's my choice, but because that's what happens when people fail at committing suicide. They're labeled as damaged and are immediately rushed off to some form of therapy in an attempt to be fixed.

"Our mom is calling," Alison says as her phone starts to ring. She walks towards the hallway, and Madison quietly follows behind her. I know them leaving means I'll be alone with Blake for a few minutes, which makes me feel nervous. The room is soon filled with an awkward, uncomfortable silence as the only sounds come from all the hospital machinery. Blake continues to stand against the wall, his eyes wandering around the room and looking anywhere but me.

The silence is overwhelming and I begin to grow anxious for noise. *I have to say something.*

"So how's school going?" My voice cracks awkwardly and I sigh, hating myself for trying to start a conversation as if everything is completely fine. Blake's eyes immediately move to me, and he just looks at me as if he's calculating how to respond. His eyes soften a bit before he responds.

"Ever since everyone found out about you, that's all they've been talking about," he admits, taking a seat next to the bed. "You know a few students said they saw you jump off the pier?"

"I bet they're all pretending to be worried for me." I scoff.

"Well, I'm not," he says before looking down. I look at him, not really thinking much about his comment. "So why'd you do it?" He looks back up at me. I let out a huff, wanting to avoid the topic as much as possible.

"I don't want t—"

"Don't, Alexa," he says. "You may be able to get away with this with my sisters, but I see through it. Something is wrong, and you need to talk to someone about it. I don't want you pushing my sisters away when they're just trying to help."

I sit there, shocked at his small outburst. What I hate the most is the fact that he's right.

"I wanted to see Cam." I keep my eyes focused on the wall in front of me. "I thought that if I jumped, then all of this would be over." I turn to see Blake and I can't tell what he's thinking. Does he even know about Cam? Surely the girls would have told him. Maybe confiding in him is a mistake.

"You would've really thrown your life away like that?" He gives me a pained expression. I think about it really well before answering. After seeing how this has affected my parents and the girls, I would hate for them to go through what I did.

"No." I shake my head. "I thought, at the moment, maybe it'd solve things, but once my body was underwater, there was this sliver of regret that remained the whole time," I say.

"They want to be there for you," he whispers. "Let them."

None of this makes sense. I don't understand why Alison and Madison are trying to be here all of a sudden, and why Blake, their brother who I didn't know existed until recently, seems to care so much either. It's even harder to understand why I feel so at ease with him when it should be the complete opposite. He gets up and walks back to his spot against the wall as my parents and the girls walk back in.

"They didn't have chicken noodle soup, so this was the second best option," my mother says as she sits next to me and opens the container filled with green liquid. My stomach churns at the sight of it.

"I'm really sorry, Alexa, but we have to go," Madison says. "Thanks for allowing us to visit," she says to my parents.

"Of course." My mother forces a smile as they come over and engulf me in a quick hug.

"I promise we'll be here tomorrow to make up for this short visit. I'm just happy you're okay," Alison whispers. I nod in response.

They make their way out of the room as Blake's green eyes linger on me for a moment. And then they're gone, leaving the room more silent than it was before.

35

CHAPTER NINE

Everything is pitch black. I look around, realizing that I'm in the water again. I begin to panic until it registers that there is no crushing pain on my chest; there's no overwhelming feeling of being suffocated because this time, I'm not drowning. I'm just . . . here.

There's a quick movement to my right, and I jerk my head to the side. At first, I couldn't see her. It's like looking through a blurry lens, but then my vision focuses and I see her. She's there, in front of me, her hair floating up all around her.

"Cam?" I try to call her name; nothing but a strangled noise and a few air bubbles come out. She looks at me with a pained expression, and I try reaching for her but I can't touch her. It's like she's here but not here at all.

She holds something out to me, and I still at the envelope with my name on it. I slowly take it from her grasp and look at it. It's identical to the one hidden in my drawer. When I look back up, she's gone, leaving me with no explanation. Just like that day.

"Alexa." My eyes snap open. It takes me a second to adjust to my surroundings. "Honey, the doctor's here to see you."

"Hi, Alexa. I'm Dr. Marin. How are you feeling?" A middle-aged woman with blonde hair, which is thrown up into a ponytail, approaches me with a clipboard in hand.

"I'm okay," I say slowly, still a little disoriented from the dream I just had. It felt so real.

"Glad to see that you've recovered. ARDS is not something most people recover from so quickly."

"ARDS?" A feeling of panic settles in the pit of my stomach.

"Acute Respiratory Distress Syndrome. It happens when fluid leaks into your lungs, blocking the oxygen from getting to your organs. You're very lucky someone found you when they did. We were able to treat it right away."

"But am I fine now?"

"Well, I just need to check your vitals but you should be okay." She smiles at me as she puts on her stethoscope and proceeds to check my heartbeat and my eyes and then my vitals.

"You are good to go, Ms. Parker." She smiles again before talking to my parents and exiting the room.

"So when are we going to go home?" I slide out of the hospital bed for the first time since I've been here, my feet making contact with the cold floor. My parents share a look and my dad clears his throat.

"Oh no." I sigh. "What is it?"

"We don't think you should go home right now." He scratches the back of his neck, and I furrow my brows in confusion.

"What do you mean I'm not going home?"

"Honey." My mother comes towards me and places her hand on my shoulder, and I begin to feel like I'm in some sort of movie. "We've been talking and doing some research. This hospital has a great program that offers—"

"You're going to put me in an asylum?" My voice raises in anger and frustration. I sit back down on the hospital bed, my heart beginning to beat faster.

"Honey, it's not an asylum. It's a program that—"

"There's nothing wrong with me!" I interrupt her explanation as my eyes begin to well up with tears. "You can't do this to me."

"Alexa, you tried to kill yourself. What do you think you're putting us through right now? Do you seriously not see that there's a problem here?" my father says sternly.

"Please don't leave me here. I promise I'll do better." I whisper, grabbing on to both of their arms.

"It's only for a week." My mother tries to keep a calm façade but even I can see how hard she's trying to fight back the tears.

"What about school?" I try to argue while wiping the tears from my eyes before they can fall.

"We'll have your friends bring your school work. I'm sure they won't mind." I clench my hands into fists and turn away from them.

"Alexa, please don't think we're doing this to punish you. We're doing this to help you. Please understand that."

"Fine," I say.

I'm angry at them for just deciding to leave me here as if I'm some burden that they can't handle, as if I'm some mental patient they need to be cautious of. Maybe what I did was crazy, but I'm not crazy. Right?

CHAPTER TEN

I feel trapped like a fragile caged animal. It has only been a day since my parents told me that I will be here for another week for "mental health help" and I feel like I'm going to go crazy. That is why I'm here, right? To make sure I'm not crazy?

"Alexa?" A nurse peeks her head through the door. "It's time for your session."

Right, because me staying here to receive help means that I also have to attend therapy sessions. Like that would actually help me.

I nod, standing up from the bed and sluggishly making my way out of the new room they moved me to. We make our way to the therapist, passing by all the rooms of people who are probably here for similar reasons. We finally approach the door labeled: Dr. Barnes M.D. The nurse knocks on the door before opening it, and I enter the large room. It's similar to my previous therapist's office; there's a large bookshelf that covers one wall along with several certificates and degrees that are hung on either side of it. Dr. Barnes is sitting on a white chair with her legs crossed and a clipboard on her lap.

She gives me a warm smile, signaling for me to take a seat on the white couch before telling the nurse to retreat. My eyes wander around the room and land on her desk in the far corner. Papers and folders are neatly piled on top of it.

"Shall we begin, Ms. Parker?" she asks, interrupting my wandering eyes. I shrug in response.

"Why don't you just start off by telling me why you're here."

"I don't know," I say, which is a lie because I know exactly why I'm here and that I probably deserve to be here. "My parents seem to think I'm crazy." I fiddle with the hem of my hoodie as I avoid eye contact.

"And do you think you're crazy?" She uses that voice that all therapists seem to use, like parents being careful not to upset their toddler. I sigh and rub my temple as I close my eyes. I don't want to be here, and I definitely don't want to be answering her stupid questions. "Alexa, the point of these sessions is so you can talk to me so I can help you. You not confiding in me is going to make things a little more difficult. So help me help you."

"Fine," I give in. "What do you want to know?"

"Why don't you tell me how you feel?" I resist the urge to scoff. I feel angry that I'm at this place. I feel like a captive animal being held in this room, and I feel broken because Cam is still gone.

"Terrible," I say. She nods and looks down at her clipboard, scribbling something down.

"What has made you feel this way?"

"Well, I don't know. Maybe it was my best friend killing herself but I'm sure you already know that."

"And you tried to kill yourself as a result of her death, correct?" I flinch at her words. My silence confirms it all, and she continues with her questions.

"Why?"

"I thought that if I died, I'd get to see her again."

"How do you feel about the fact that you're still alive?"

This session is starting to get pointless and my patience is thinning.

"How exactly is this supposed to help me?" I spit out. "Do you really think that reminding me of her death and how I failed to kill myself is going to solve all my problems?"

I don't look at her as I get up and make my way towards the door. She doesn't bother to stop me either as I leave. I push my way past a few hospital staff and push the door of my room open.

"Oh good, you're back!" Alison throws the magazine she's reading on the nightstand and stands up from her spot on the bed.

"What are you guys doing here? Not that I'm not happy to see you, but why didn't you guys tell me you were coming?" I enter the room and close the door behind me.

"We texted you but it seems you left your phone here," Madison starts. "Your parents asked us to bring you your school work." My eyes drift to the small stack of papers next to the magazine and then they drift to Blake.

"And why are you here?" I question and he looks up from his phone.

"Well, that idiot over there," he motions towards Madison, "crashed their car, and now, I have the pleasure of driving them around."

"Oh shut up, Blake. You said you wanted to come anyway." I turn my attention back to Blake, raising my eyebrows. He quickly shakes his head and denies their accusations.

"Anyways, how is it here?" Alison questions. Her eyes wander around the small room, and I begin to feel ashamed.

"It feels like I'm suffocating in a box." I sigh. "They have me locked up here for hours except for therapy sessions."

They give me a sorry look, which doesn't really help, but I appreciate it all the same.

"So how's school been without me?" I inquire, confused when they all share a look.

"Uh, it's been good," Madison says unsurely, which only adds to my suspicion.

"What's going on?" I ask, growing a bit annoyed.

Blake sighs and rolls his eyes. "They don't want to tell you that you've been the talk of the school."

"What do you mean?"

"Well, when the news came back of why you haven't been at school and what happened to you, Paige saw it as her cue to tell everyone that you're crazy." My eyes widen and a feeling of dread settles in my stomach.

"Of course she did. I just don't understand why she hates me so much." And of course everyone wanted to know about the girl who fell from the top of the social hierarchy.

"You're everything she's not. I see why she'd hate you," Alison states.

"Yeah." Madison bites her lip. "We've been trying to defend you but it's us three against the school." I nod, thanking them for at least trying to protect me.

"We're going to go find a bathroom," Alison says after a few moments, taking Madison with her. My eyes flicker to Blake's, whose eyes are already on mine.

"Do they have some twin bladder problem?" I ask.

"Hospitals make them nervous. They also feel bad about what happened."

Nodding, I make my way to my bed and turn on the small television that I'm surprised is even in the room.

"So how's therapy going?" I stop channel-surfing and just opt to turn the television off.

"Considering the fact that I walked out mid-session today, I'd say it's going great." He laughs at my sarcasm.

"And the worst thing about being here is that everything is about her. She's the topic of my therapy sessions. She's what every nurse mentions. She's the reason why I'm here. No matter how much I want to be angry at her, I can't help but feel like it's all my fault."

He stays silent for a moment. "It's not your fault," he says. Just then the girls burst through the door with Alison doubling over in laughter.

"Madison tripped on the way here in front of some hot nurse, and it was hilarious," she cackles, which explains why Madison is glaring daggers at her.

I try not to laugh for Madison's sake, but then Blake joins Alison, and it's as if their laughter is infectious because I can't help but join in too. So I laugh—really laugh—and I can't help but think about how I haven't laughed this hard in a while.

CHAPTER ELEVEN

Boredom has become my worst enemy. I stare out the window located at the far end of the room, only to be met with a brick wall that hides whatever view is on the other side. I pay no mind to the knock on the door; it's probably one of the nurses dropping off my evening meal. The room is deafeningly silent except for the sound of the second hand ticking on the clock—a sound I've already grown to hate.

Another knock resounds through the room, and I begin to grow annoyed. I march towards the door, yanking it open to reveal a stunned Blake with his fist in the air, ready to knock again. I furrow my eyebrows at seeing him alone but I step aside, allowing him to enter the room.

"Where are the girls?" I ask as he takes a seat on one of the chairs next to my bed and places a small stack of papers on to the nightstand.

"They have the flu so they told me to come drop off your work," he replies. "And they also made me bring you this. It's a bagel and brownie, I believe." He pulls out a paper bag, which he must have sneaked in here seeing as the nurses don't allow outside food.

"Oh thank god!" I grab the bag out of his hand and open it. "I swear these hospitals want to starve people with the food they provide." He laughs at my comment.

"How was your day?" he questions. I realize how weird this all is—how he manages to keep making appearances in my life. I can't quite figure out what his intentions are, and why he seems to care so much, but oddly enough, I feel comfortable with him around.

"Okay, I guess," I reply.

"What do you do all day here?"

"Well, I sleep, stare out the window, catch up on my work, eat, and shower," I start. "Basically, what I do at home except I'm forced to do those things here along with attending therapy."

"At least you're not missing out on anything at school." He shrugs. I start to remember the first time they visited; it was when I found out about Paige's rumors, and the now familiar feeling of dread settles into the pit of my stomach.

"Have the rumors gotten worse?"

"Not really." He shakes his head. "Some girl's picture got sent around the school and that's kind of the new buzz." I sigh in relief at the fact that people have stopped talking about me for now, but I can't help but feel sorry for that girl. She must feel terrible, but this is how society works. People are quick to judge you, but forget about you just as fast when something else grabs their attention.

"What happened to your hand?" I ask, noticing him rubbing his bruised knuckles. He quickly tries to hide it by crossing his arms.

"What are you talking about?"

"Seriously, Blake? Your hand is all bruised." I give him a threatening look. He gives in, uncrossing his arms and laying them out for me to see. They look as if they collided with a hard surface.

"The other day, some guy in the locker room brought up the topic of you being here," he starts. "He said that you were probably the freaky type and how he's always wanted to get a piece of you ever since he saw you in that cheer uniform, and he said a whole lot of other stuff about you." I look down in embarrassment.

"So how did you injure your hand?" I ask after a moment of silence and he sighs.

"I told him to stop talking about you like that when he doesn't even know your situation, and he got mad and shoved me against the lockers. So I punched him in the face." My eyes widen at the explanation.

"Why did you defend me?"

"Because no one deserves to be talked about like that. Not after all you've been through. Plus, Alison and Madison would kill me if they found out I didn't do anything." A warm feeling washes over me. I can't help the smile that finds its way on to my face. At that moment, I don't feel like I want to disappear. After Blake left, a nurse came to collect me for my session with Dr. Barnes. I was irritated throughout the whole session, but I promised my parents that I won't walk out again. When I get back to my room, they are there waiting for me. My mother sets her phone down on the nightstand.

"What are you guys doing here?" I ask.

"What do you mean? You're our daughter, and we're here to make sure you're okay," my father replies as he makes an attempt to engulf me in a hug, but I step away, not at all feeling guilty as hurt flashes in his eyes.

I find it hard to believe that they even care about me at all. They put me here, and if they really did care, they would've brought me back home where I can recover in comfort instead of paying some "professional" to watch over me for them.

"Alexa, how are you feeling today?" my mother questions and I roll my eyes.

"Hm, let me think about how I feel about being locked in a room all day and being forced to attend pointless therapy sessions just so you guys can make sure I don't want to try to kill myself again."

"Alexa, I know you don't understand why we're doing this, but that's a bit ridiculous, don't you think?" my father says when words can't seem to make their way out of my mother's mouth.

"Why don't you try being in here for a week?"

"Where is this coming from?" my mother screams. "I don't like your attitude!"

"Well then, it's a good thing you don't have to deal with it, right?" I scream back, feeling my eyes start to water. "I bet you guys have been much happier without having me around."

"Alexa, don't star—" my father begins, but before he can finish his sentence, my mother cuts him off.

"How can you even say that?" Tears are brimming her eyes, which makes me even angrier.

"Just admit it, you guys don't care about me because if you did, you wouldn't have put me here in the first place. I don't belong here!" At this point, the tears are rolling down my cheeks. My mother starts crying, too, but I don't feel a sliver of remorse for yelling at them. My own parents can't even be here for me after Cam's death. They don't understand. My mother looks at me for a moment with her tear-filled eyes before storming out of the room, my father going after her. I find myself furiously wiping my eyes as I make my way to the bed. *What's happening to me?*

CHAPTER TWELVE

"How are you feeling today, Ms. Parker?" Dr. Barnes takes her usual seat before me, asking the same question that, by now, I'm tired of being asked. It's my second to last day here and this is my last therapy session.

"Same as always." I sigh, slumping onto the sofa. I hate having to attend these sessions with a passion, but since I'm planning on leaving in a day, I decide to just suck it up.

"And have you continued to have any thoughts about harming yourself?"

"No," I answer honestly. Being underwater for so long and not being able to breathe was the worst feeling ever.

"How do you feel about Cameron?" She looks up at me from her clipboard, waiting for an answer.

"Well, considering the fact that she's still dead and how everyone seems to make it their mission to constantly remind me of her, I'd say I'm fantastic." The sarcasm hides the hint of sadness that comes as I think about her.

"Ms. Parker, I know this type of thing is difficult to cope with," she starts and I scoff.

"Please, what would you know?" I spit out. "You don't know what it feels like to lose the only person who understood you. You don't know what it feels like to be so alone and helpless that even your own parents and friends can't do anything about it."

"That's where you're wrong." She raises her voice, silencing me. "Three years ago, I lost my husband to suicide. He was a war veteran," she says, taking a deep breath. My body goes rigid at her confession.

"I'm sorry for your loss," I whisper, suddenly feeling horrible for my hostility towards her these past few days. "How'd you deal with it?"

"I talked about it, believe it or not. I found someone else to trust and I talked and told them how I felt," she replies.

"Did it get better?"

"Yes," she says sincerely. "It took some time, but I realized that it wasn't my fault. Maybe I could have stopped it, and maybe I could have noticed what he was going through, but I didn't and that's something you have to accept." I don't respond, and as much I hate to admit it, she's right.

"Alexa," she calls me by my first name, and I look at her—really look at her. "It's not your fault. Cam had a reason for doing what she did, and instead of being angry at her, you have to be grateful for the time you got to spend with her." I stay quiet for a minute, her words repeating themselves in my head.

"Thank you," I whisper. I didn't realize the harm I caused to myself until now. She nods back at me before her timer goes off, signaling the end of the session. I stand up from my seat, thanking Dr. Barnes before slowly making my way back to my room.

When I enter my room, I'm still in a daze. My mind is going over what Dr. Barnes said. That's when I have an epiphany. Cam is gone, really gone, and she isn't ever going to come back. Me trying to hold onto her as if she'll walk into my arms any day now has caused my life to go down a dark tunnel—one that I wouldn't be able to get out of alone. I have to accept her death, and I have to accept everything that has happened following her death.

* * *

I sit by the window the next morning, staring at nothing but that brick wall. Today is the day that I finally leave this place, and I grow anxious. I can only imagine the whispers and gossip that will, without a doubt, spread upon my return, but I'm also nervous to face my parents. I haven't seen them since my outburst, and I wonder if they'll even bother to come get me and bring me home. I turn my attention to the door when I hear a knock on the door, and I almost sigh in relief when my parents walk in. My mother rushes to me embracing me in a hug and I release a breath I didn't realize I was holding. It feels so good being in her arms. She pulls away, giving me a sincere smile before allowing my father to hug me.

"Mom, I'm sorry," I speak, not being able to act okay with them if I don't apologize first. "To you too, Dad." I turn to him. "What I said was out of line and I shouldn't have disrespected you guys like that." My mother cups my face and tucks loose strands of hair behind my ears.

"It's okay, honey." She kisses me on my forehead. "Now, let's get you out of here."

Upon arriving home, I rush inside and inhale the familiar scent of home. My parents follow a few minutes later, carrying the duffel bag that contains the very few clothing items I brought when I was staying at the hospital.

"Alexa, lunch will be ready soon," my mother yells from the kitchen. I rest my head on one of the decorative pillows we bought with the couch and switch on the television. My father sits in the chair beside me and watches some teenage drama with me, even letting out a chuckle here and there at the silly jokes. I can't help the grin that makes an appearance on my face.

For the first time since Cam died, it feels like everything is going to be okay. It feels like things are going back to normal. My parents don't pressure me to talk about how I feel or what I learned from my time at the hospital, and I'm appreciative of that. It will still take me a while to fill in that empty void Cam left, but I'm getting better and I'm finally ready to face my problems.

CHAPTER THIRTEEN

It's the Wednesday before Thanksgiving, and the kitchen is littered with grocery bags containing a plethora of ingredients, one of them being a massive turkey.

"Oh, you're up!" My mother smiles in surprise as she walks into the kitchen with her hands holding up multiple aluminum trays.

"I'm feeling a lot better," I reply. "What's all this for?" I ask, referring to the grocery store that's sitting on our counters.

"It's for the party, silly." She chuckles, reminding me of tomorrow.

Thanksgiving is the day when families reunite. The day where you have to sit down and act as if everything is perfect in life. The day when you have to suck up your hatred towards the world and everyone you dislike and be thankful. Thanksgiving for my family means a huge get together where all their coworkers and friends flood our house, bringing store-bought pumpkin pies and fruitcakes. Oh, and let's not forget the endless bottles of cheap wine.

Ever since Cam's death, I've had very little to be grateful for. Call me over dramatic, but the world took the one person I trust, and I'm supposed to say thank you? I don't think so.

Therefore, this Thanksgiving, I will be spending the whole night locked away in my comfortable room instead of being forced to interact with all of the fake strangers and distant relatives.

"Oh right," I reply to my mother who now has her whole forearm deep inside the turkey.

I cringe at the deceased bird as I exit the kitchen before being stopped by my mother.

"Have you invited your friends for tomorrow?"

"Mom, they have families, you know." I roll my eyes standing with my back towards her.

"I'm glad you said that." She giggles. "Because I ran into Alison and Madison's mother at the store and invited her whole family," she announces.

"You what?" My eyes widen as I turn to face her.

Alison and Madison aren't the only children in that family. The Harpers being invited means there's a chance Blake will show up as well. I suddenly feel a peculiar feeling in my stomach at the thought of Blake being here. Parties and I are not a good mix, and the last thing I need is him seeing a possible breakdown of mine, and this time in front of a large audience.

"Please relax, Alexa. We'll get to fully meet your new friends!" she shrieks excitedly. I don't reply and, instead, groan as I stomp to my room.

*   *   *

The next day, the doorbell rings continually as friends and family begin to flood the house. I take that as my cue to go upstairs and avoid confrontation. I look in the mirror, making some last minute adjustments to my makeup and outfit. The Harpers will be here soon, and my heart is beating faster by the second. All I have to do is get through tonight without making a fool of myself. I pace across my room, inhaling and exhaling deeply until I'm interrupted by yelling from downstairs.

"Alexa! Get down here and say hello to the Harpers!"

I freeze in front of my door, my anxiety levels going bonkers. I finally manage to move and slowly creep down the stairs until I stand before the Harpers. The girls are quick to squeal and embrace me in a hug as they attack me with compliments to which I smile before moving on to greet Mr. and Mrs. Harper who sweetly ask me how I'm doing to which I lie and say that I'm great. I turn away from the couple, instantly colliding with a hard body and stumble back.

"Happy Thanksgiving to you too?" Blake greets in the form of a question.

"Hey," I breathe, giving him a slight smile, which he reciprocates.

We both keep eye contact for what feels like minutes but is actually only for a few seconds. I'm surprised yet grateful that it doesn't feel awkward at all. That is until my mother speaks up, breaking the silence. I sheepishly smile, trying to shake off the tension that has built and follow my mother as she shows them to the dining room where all the food and refreshments are. It's been half an hour, and as more friends and family arrive, I find myself upstairs with the girls as they question me about the "stare off" between Blake and I.

"Nothing is going on!" I laugh incredulously at how delusional the two are.

"We saw the way he looked at you, Alexa!" Madison lifts one of her perfectly plucked eyebrows.

"Guys, Blake and I barely talk," I state, brushing off their silly ideas. "Plus I'm pretty sure he's scared of me because of everything that's happened."

Ever since the day at the pier, it's like everyone makes sure to be cautious of me. Like I'm surrounded by shards of glass, and the only way to make sure that there isn't another incident is to be extra cautious around me.

"Seriously, Alexa?" Madison questions in disbelief and Alison joins in.

"Do you really think he would've come with us to visit you all those times if he was scared of you?" They did have a point, but then again, it's Thanksgiving. I doubt he had a choice in the matter.

"Okay but still," I reply. "You guys are making something out of nothing." The two roll their eyes at me before changing the subject. We begin by talking about the upcoming winter formal our school holds every year. It's one of the many nights where girls get to dress up and dance in a smelly school gymnasium for the night.

I remember how Cam and I would always go. She would always show up wearing sneakers with her dress instead of heels, and I admired her for it. We would spend the night making fools of ourselves on the dance floor and laughing at anyone who gave us dirty looks. I even remember Cam almost getting in a fight one time after a girl told her she couldn't dance. I almost laugh out loud when I think about how she also ended up making out with the same girl's boyfriend.

"Alexa, you're crying." Madison snaps me out of my trance, and I quickly begin wiping away the tears that start to fall.

"Sorry." I sniffle. "I was just thinking about something."

"Cam?" she asks.

"Yeah." I sigh.

"We miss her too." Alison gives me a sad smile as she takes a seat next to me on my bed.

It's been almost two months already yet it feels like I received the news this morning.

Life is so unpredictable. One day, everything you love and care about can be ripped away from you, and you just have to deal with it. I miss my best friend, but I'm grateful for the time I had with her even if it was cut way too short. I look at the two girls who are both trying their best to comfort me, and at that moment, I realize I have only been pushing them away when I should've been grateful to have the two of them.

The door bursts open, and the girls and I jump, trying to compose ourselves before whoever enters can sense that something is wrong in the first place.

"Alexa! It's your—" The two people I least expect enter the room and I immediately roll my eyes.

"Woah! Hello, beautiful ladies." My cousins Caleb and Braden, who happen to be twins, gawk at the sight of Alison and Madison. I groan in annoyance.

"What do you guys want?" I question.

"I think the real question is, why haven't you introduced us to your lovely friends?" Caleb flashes them a smile, and I look to see that Alison and Madison are both blushing.

Are you kidding me? It hasn't even been two minutes, and they're already falling for their charms.

"Caleb and Braden, this is Alison and Madison. Alison and Madison, these idiots are my cousins Caleb and Braden," I introduce quickly. "There. Now, get out."

"Actually, your mom sent us up here and told us to tell you to get your butt downstairs and stop being so antisocial," Braden states.

"We have been up here for a while," Madison points out.

"Fine," I say. We all head downstairs where the girls are immediately swept away by dumb and dumber.

All of these people are making me anxious, and I wonder if I can find a way to sneak back up to my room again where I can be alone. I walk into the kitchen where all the adults are laughing as they sip from their wine glasses.

"Alexa, darling, how are you?" My aunt Katherine asks as she pulls me in for a hug; I don't hug back. I pull away, gradually making my way to the living room. I'm hoping to successfully make a run for it and spend the rest of the night in the sanctuary of my room.

"Not a fan of family gatherings?" Blake asks from behind me, making me jump in my place.

"Well, considering my family talks about everyone behind their backs . . . nope, not a fan." He chuckles at my attitude towards my relatives.

"So what are you thankful for? Besides your loving family, of course," he jokes to which I reply with a genuine laugh.

"I don't know." I shrug, scared that he will judge me for my words. I'm proved wrong when he nods in understanding.

"That's fair," he replies. "I would feel the same after going through everything you have."

"Dinner's ready!" my mother yells from the kitchen, and we both stand up from our spots on the couch. Before he walks into the kitchen, I stop him.

"What are you thankful for?" I ask. He turns to me, remaining silent for a second before replying.

"My sisters," he starts. "And for them meeting you," he finishes before turning on his heel and disappearing into the dining room.

I can't really describe what I feel in that moment. I shake it off, making my way to the dining room only to find that all the seats are already filled except the one between Blake and Alison. I glare at her, knowing exactly what she's doing. I take my seat, unfolding the napkin on my lap.

"Okay, everyone. Let's say grace," my mother announces, signaling to take your neighbors' hands and bow your head down in prayer. I look at Blake who only gives me a small smile, extending his hand. I smile back, placing my hand in his and bowing my head. My mom leads the prayer while I add in my own, praying that my hand doesn't begin to sweat. After a few minutes, we all say "Amen" and detach our hands.

"Let's eat!" my mother cheers.

* * *

Alison and Madison ditch me once again after dinner, choosing to go for a walk with Caleb and Braden. To be fair, they did invite me, but after eating so much food, I'm feeling up to it. So now here I am, stuck in a corner while the grown-ups sit down by the kitchen island, eating dessert while skimming through my embarrassing baby pictures.

My cheeks are bright red in humiliation from all the "look at those cheeks!" coming from my mother. She sounds like she's had one too many glasses of wine with her excessive giggling. I decide to abandon my spot and head outside to the now empty backyard. It's a beautiful night with all the shimmering lights that my mother thought will be a nice touch. I sit down on the wooden bench we've had out here since I was a toddler and take a deep breath, taking in the peace and quiet.

"It's nice out here," Blake says. He takes a seat next to me, and I scoot over to give him some more room.

"Yeah, I guess it is," I reply. "What are you doing out here?"

"Just wanted to check in on you since my sisters seem to have abandoned you," he says humorously. I don't say anything and we just sit in silence for a while.

"What does it feel like?" he asks suddenly. I look at him, furrowing my brows.

"What does what feel like?"

"Losing someone so close to you." A feeling of sadness rushes over me as I think about it.

"I'm sorry, I shouldn't have—"

"No, it's okay," I interrupt. "I don't know. I guess it's like this sudden emptiness. The feeling that you're not completely whole anymore." He doesn't say anything, he just looks at me and I continue. "It's like drowning while everyone around you is breathing." I think about being underwater again. The peacefulness of it all at first and then the crushing pain and realization of what's happening.

"What hurts even worse is not even knowing why. Cam just left me with no explanation, and all I have left of her is some stupid letter that I'm too scared to read." The moment those words leave my mouth, I instantly regret it. I haven't told anyone about the letter, not even Alison and Madison.

I start to worry that I've scared Blake off because he's still quiet. "You should read it. Read the letter," he says.

My eyes start to water and I pull him into a hug, blinking the tears away.

"Thank you for listening," I whisper. When we pull away, he's staring at me with those beautiful green eyes. I can't help it as I stare back.

Before I know it, he's kissing me. At first, I'm completely still, shocked that this is actually happening. I can feel him hesitating, but before he can pull away, I wrap my arms around his neck as I close my eyes and kiss him back. A euphoric feeling settles over me, and I can't believe that I'm kissing Blake Harper. The kiss is gentle and sweet, and I don't know how long it's been but I know that I don't want the kiss to end.

And then it all hits me. I'm Alexa Parker, the girl whose best friend committed suicide, the girl who gave up everything, and the girl who wanted to end her own life because she's hopeless and doesn't want to handle it on her own. I shouldn't be doing this. I shouldn't be kissing Blake because a boy like Blake doesn't deserve to be with a girl like me, and he definitely doesn't deserve to take on all the baggage I come with. I snap my eyes open, and I push away from him, my breathing erratic and my heart thumping loudly in my chest as I stand up.

"Alexa—" he starts, but I cut him off, not trusting myself to be around him for a second longer.

"I'm sorry. I need to go," I say as I walk away from the sweetest guy I have ever met . . . with no explanation.

CHAPTER FOURTEEN

I step out of my car, shutting the door behind me and slowly approaching the entrance to the school. Unfortunately, Thanksgiving break means nothing when it comes to drama at my school, and I know that the gossip mill will resume turning as soon as I step foot into that hallway.

Fortunately for me, the most I get are stares as I make my way to my locker. I haven't talked to Alison and Madison since Thanksgiving, and I definitely haven't talked to Blake, not that I even want to. In fact, it will probably be easier if I don't see him at all. Every time I think about the kiss we shared, an unsettling feeling appears in my stomach. I'm not sure how I feel about it, but as soon as I left him in my backyard that night, I decided that it will be best to just erase whatever happened between us from my memory.

Someone's leaning against the locker next to mine, and I stiffen as I realize it's Paige. I really hope she uses that brain of hers and walks away because I am so not ready to deal with her crap.

"How was rehab, Alexa?" she asks cloyingly. I roll my eyes, seeing as that's probably where the whole school thought I was. I ignore her and start to take out my books for my first few classes, which only makes her irritated.

"I'm surprised they even let you out considering—" she continues, but someone cuts her off.

"Do you have an off switch?" Alison asks angrily as she and Madison make their way to my side.

"Do you always have to be such a prick? Like seriously, what did she ever do to you?" Madison adds. I try to contain a smile at the expression on Paige's face. Before she can say anything, the bell rings. I shut my locker before walking off with the girls not too far behind.

"Thanks for that," I say to the both of them. "I really did not want to get detention on my first day back."

"Alexa, we need to talk," Alison says; the tone of her voice makes me stop in my tracks. *Oh no*, I think. She knows about what happened that night. The warning bell rings, signaling that if you don't get to class now, you'll be late.

"We'll see you at lunch," she says, sighing. I watch as she and Madison walk away in the opposite direction, and I can't help the feeling of dread that surges over me like a wave.

* * *

I never thought I would say this, but I've never been as happy as I am now to have the arms on the classroom clock tick what would have been agonizingly slow if this is like any other day. I'm dreading going to lunch. I'm dreading having to hear what Alison and Madison want to talk to me about, and most of all, I'm dreading running into Blake.

The bell rings, snapping me out of my panicked state. I gather my things as I walk off to art history. The only reason anyone ever actually pays attention in this class is because our teacher is straight out of college and everyone thinks he's hot, but I actually like learning about art history. His lecture on the importance of the renaissance is interrupted by a knock on the door.

"Come in!" he calls out to whoever is outside. The door opens and in steps the one person I'm hoping to avoid today: Blake Harper.

"Mr. Harper," Mr. Williams greets. "What brings you to my class?"

Blake doesn't reply but instead holds up a pass with a message written on it.

"Ah." Mr. Williams takes the note from his hand before walking to his desk and retrieving a set of keys. He grabs a pen from his mug and signs the note.

Blake's eyes travel around the room of teens who take this interruption as an opportunity to talk. I look down at my book and look up again, instantly regretting it once my eyes lock on to Blake's. His face is blank of any emotion, and it's impossible to tell what's going through his mind. Before he has the chance to react, Mr. Williams is handing him the note with the keys and ordering him to get back to class. I don't notice my rapid heartbeat until he's gone. I take a sip from my water bottle, trying my best to pay attention as Mr. Williams resumes his lesson.

An hour later, I slowly make my way towards the cafeteria. I consider taking off and heading home early to avoid whatever the girls are going to say, but decide that the right thing to do is to accept that they know about what happened between Blake and I.

I haven't seen Blake around since he walked into my art history class, and the fact that I'm hiding from him like a wanted criminal would from the cops is probably a factor. My nerves are erratic as I approach the table where the girls are sitting. They're fixing their lip gloss with their phone cameras as mirrors. I take a seat at the table with all the guilt building up inside of me. I don't know why I feel guilty. I look down at my shaking leg.

"Oh, Alexa!" Madison chirps, causing Alison to look up at me with a smile. I admit that I'm confused by their light demeanor.

"So you guys wanted to talk to me?" I mumble, not being able to make eye contact.

"Oh yeah!" Alison remembers, completely oblivious to my discomfort. All my thoughts are jumbled together in my mind, and I can feel the word vomit threatening to spill.

"So we wanted to ask you abou—"

"Yes, I kissed Blake!" I blurt, my eyes widening as soon as the words escape my mouth. They're completely taken aback as their mouths hang agape. I can't help the feeling of stupidity that comes over me once I realize that probably isn't the topic of the matter.

"You what?!" they scream in unison. I sigh, putting my head down on the table while they shriek in happiness. *Why are they happy about this?*

My head shoots back up in confusion at their reaction. They have wide smiles on their faces as if they can't believe it. I don't blame them; I can hardly believe it myself.

"When did this happen?" Alison asks first.

"Thanksgiving." I bite my bottom lip anxiously.

"And why did you wait until now to tell us this?" Madison butts in.

"I don't know." I shrug. "I guess it's because I wasn't sure what it meant then and I'm still not sure what it means now."

"Well, have you talked to Blake?" Alison inquires.

"No! The last thing I want is to see him."

"Who is him?" A familiar voice enters the conversation, and I turn around to see Blake standing beside the table, looking directly at me. My stomach instantly drops at the sight of him.

This is the moment I've been trying to avoid all day, and regardless of my efforts, it's happening.

"Hi." I awkwardly wave to him, giving him a smile that I hope doesn't betray my true emotions.

"Hey," he breathes out, smiling slightly. He places his tray of food on the table before taking a seat next to Alison. "So what are we talking about?"

"We were talking about the party we have planned for Saturday," I speak up, desperate for a subject change. The two girls look at me confused but later catch on.

"Oh yeah!" Madison replies while Alison does the same after.

"Really?" he asks, narrowing his eyes at me. I nod, trying my best to seem convincing. Given by his nod, he believes it.

"Alright then. So I assume I'm invited." He raises a brow. I can't say no because then, he will definitely know I'm lying.

"Of course," I mumble, sighing in defeat.

"Cool. I'm sure my sisters will tell me the details," he replies before standing up from his seat and leaving the table. I turn to Alison and Madison who both have bewildered looks on their faces.

"Alexa!" Alison whisper-shouts with a worried look on her face. "What are you gonna do?"

"I don't know!" I whisper-shout back as the bell rings, signaling it's time to get to my next class. I stand from the table, saying a frantic goodbye to the girls before walking off to health science.

I could have easily said something else, but this is what happens when you don't think before you speak. Why did things have to be so complicated? Why did Blake have to push his way into every aspect of my life? Why did he have to kiss me? I have to nip this in the bud before it starts to grow out of my control. I can't handle another big change in my life, especially since I am still adjusting to the new path I have been thrown on and trying to accept the events that led me here.

CHAPTER FIFTEEN

I inhale the calming scent of salt water as I stand by the pier. School ended about an hour ago. Instead of going home, I find myself here, watching as the water overlaps in small waves, glistening in the sun. I probably shouldn't be here right now considering what happened the last time I was here, but I need somewhere to clear my mind and this is oddly the first place that I can think of.

I replay today's events in my mind, and I honestly don't know how or what to feel. I told on myself to the girls about the kiss with Blake, and apparently, I'm throwing a party, and things between Blake and I are more complicated than before. *How did I get here?* A gust of wind blows by, and I sigh as I push my hair out of my face.

"Alexa." My body stills at the sound of Blake's voice. I can practically feel my heart drop to the bottom of my stomach. Why is it that he's always making an appearance when I don't want him to?

"Blake." I try to hide the nervousness in my voice as I turn to him. "What are you still doing here?"

"I had lacrosse practice. I was just about to leave but I saw you here." My eyes quickly survey him. I notice the lacrosse stick in his hand and then the muscle tee he's wearing, which is practically clinging to him, the sweat on his shirt carving out every detail of his chest. I quickly avert my gaze, looking anywhere but at him.

"I needed a quiet place to think," I finally reply. We're both silent for what feels like minutes but is actually only seconds before he asks the question I've been dreading since that night.

"Alexa, can we talk?"

"There's nothing to talk about." I'm still not looking at him when I mumble those words. He lightly grabs my hand, making me look at him.

"You can't just pretend that what happened that night didn't happen." His tone is serious as his ocean eyes pierce into mine. No matter how badly I want to put what happened between us aside and try my best to forget it, I just can't.

"Blake, I just got caught in the moment and—"

"But I didn't," he interrupts, making me shut up. "I didn't kiss you because it seemed like the right thing to do at the time. I kissed you because I wanted to, and I'm sorry if I overstepped that night and made you feel uncomfortable, but I'm not going to lie and say I don't feel something for you."

My heart jumps at his words. *He feels something for me.* Blake Harper feels something for me, and it only makes me more disappointed. Not in him but in myself. I will be lying if I say I didn't feel something that night, too, but Blake deserves someone who isn't collateral damage to themselves and inevitably others. I'm not good for him, and it's best to stop this—whatever this is—from going anywhere before someone gets hurt.

"Look, we were alone outside at night, and we were having a personal conversation. I'm sure you just thought you felt something, but sooner or later, you'll find out that you never really did and it was a spur-of-the-moment thing." I sigh, ending the conversation. I begin making my way towards my car, trying to ignore the feeling of Blake's lingering gaze.

* * *

"So, Alexa, your father and I have to attend a convention this weekend for my job," my mother says, breaking me out of whatever trance I'm in. I haven't been able to eat my dinner thinking about what Blake said and about the party I'm supposed to be throwing because of him—a party that isn't going to happen.

"I'm sorry, what was that?" I reply, not sure if I heard her words correctly.

"I said your father and I will be at a convention this weekend," she repeats while taking a sip of her wine. "We'll be back Sunday afternoon."

I nod in response, agreeing to not burn the house down in their absence or do anything stupid. I know they're worried about leaving me home alone for the weekend, or more specifically of what I can do if I'm left alone, but they really want to fully trust me again and I'm going to prove to them that they can. I pick at my food, my appetite suddenly gone. Soon, I pick up my plate, discarding my food into the trash bin and heading up to bed. After showering and brushing my teeth, I crawl under my duvet, hoping to get some sleep. Instead, I find myself thinking about the dark-haired boy who admitted his feelings for me earlier today. The thought of him reminds me of how much I need to forget him and how much I need to forget I ever felt anything that night too.

* * *

"Ms. Parker." Mr. Williams wakes me up from my nap. "Since you seem to love this class so much, I'm sure you won't mind joining me for lunch to help grade some papers." I roll my eyes as everyone laughs at his sarcastic comment. I begin putting my stuff away given that there are only two minutes left of class. Once the bell rings, I bolt out of the room and make my way to my last class before lunch.

The rest of the period consists of doing a worksheet silently, and before I know it, the bell is ringing. I get out of my seat, making my way to Mr. Williams' room. The room is empty except for Mr. Williams who's focused on grading papers. I clear my throat, making my presence known. His eyes flicker up to mine.

"Oh, Ms. Parker." He grins. "Why don't you take a seat, and you can help me grade some of these papers." I nod, sitting down at the desk in front of him as he sets a fair stack of papers in front of me along with the rubric. I start by reading the first paper on the stack, rolling my eyes at the name at the top of the paper. Blake Harper. *Can I catch a break?*

The essay is on the importance of the renaissance, and I marvel at how great of a writer he is. A feeling of guilt begins to take over me. I find myself not being able to focus on grading his paper. A part of me wants to talk to Blake but the other part of me knows that I shouldn't.

"So, Ms. Parker . . ." Mr. Williams starts, pulling me away from all thoughts of Blake. "Have you applied to any colleges yet?" His question takes me by surprise as college isn't something I've had the privilege of thinking about lately. He looks at me expectantly and I shake my head.

"Um . . . no," I say. "Unfortunately, I haven't really had the time to think about college these past few weeks." I'm sure he's heard about what's happened these past few months. I wait for him to give me that look of pity but he doesn't. Instead, he gives me a reassuring smile.

"Well, I'm sure you'll figure that out before graduation," he says. "In fact, I didn't know which career path I wanted to take until my sophomore year of college. I thought I wanted to be a doctor, but here I am, teaching art history to a bunch of high school students not even half my age." We both laugh at that.

It's no secret that Mr. Williams is a really good looking guy and, because he's in his early twenties, girls at this school go crazy over him. Especially Cam.

"He's so hot," Cam *says as she watches him grab a snack from the vending machine.*

"Let's not forget that he's your teacher," I remind her with a smirk on my face.

"Ugh, how unfortunate." He catches us watching him. We both duck our heads while bursting into laughter.

I close my eyes, my heart aching at the memory.

"Ms. Parker, are you alright?" Mr. Williams questions and I quickly nod.

"Yeah, I just remembered I have to do something really important. I'm sorry. May I go?"

"Sure. Lunch is about to end soon anyway." I grab my bag and head towards the door.

"Oh, and try not to fall asleep in my class again," he calls out before I exit.

CHAPTER SIXTEEN

Looking at colleges is hard, especially when you don't even know what you want to do with your life. Talking with Mr. Williams made me realize that I should really take back control of my life and start preparing for my future, but that's the thing. How am I supposed to prepare for the future when I don't know what I'm preparing myself for?

"So have you decided what you're going to do for the party you told Blake you're having?" Alison questions as she takes a sip of her vanilla bean frappe. The girls begged me to go to Starbucks with them after school as they feel like we aren't spending enough time together.

"My parents are coincidentally going to be out of town this weekend, but I'm not so sure throwing a party is the best idea," I reply.

"If you don't have the party, then Blake is going to know you're lying," Madison states.

"He probably wouldn't even care if I had a party or not, plus I'm pretty sure he knows we were talking about him. He just wanted me to admit it."

"Okay. Well, then maybe you really shouldn't throw a party. How about we have a movie night?" Alison suggests.

"And maybe you can invite your hot cousins." Madison wiggles her eyebrows at me and I laugh.

"Yes to the movie night and no to inviting my idiot cousins."

"You're no fun," they say simultaneously, causing all of us to erupt in giggles.

I don't fail to notice my father's absence when my mother calls me down for dinner later that night. He's starting to work late nights again, and I figure it will be best to just stop asking for him and let him work on his case.

"How was school?" my mother asks, attempting a conversation.

"School is school." I sigh.

"Well, your teachers have been keeping me updated. They are saying that you're doing really well and that you should be able to get back on track very soon."

"I was thinking . . ." I start, changing the topic. "This weekend since you and dad are going to be out of town and I'll be by myself for a few days, maybe I can have some friends over to keep me company."

"That's a great idea!" she says immediately.

I know she will say yes. I know my parents are afraid of leaving me at home by myself, more out of fear of what they could possibly come home to.

"Great!" I reply. "I'm going to head upstairs and call it a night."

"Alright, honey. Goodnight." I clear my plate and head up to my room as I text the girls to tell them that the plans for this weekend are a go.

The next day goes by surprisingly smoothly. I don't fall asleep in any of my classes, and I am successfully able to switch out of poetry, which the girls aren't too happy about as it's the only class I have with them. It's also the only class I have with Blake who is kind of the reason I switched out of that class in the first place. I know it kind of sounds extreme for me to do that, but things are just easier when I'm not around him. When the bell rings, signaling that school is over, I sigh in relief. The parking lot is littered with teens as I make my way to my car, wanting to leave the premises without getting stuck in student traffic.

I make my way to the spot I have been going to every day after school this week—the pier. The moment is perfect. The sun is partly hidden by clouds and a cool, crisp wind blows across the water.

"Wanna skip some rocks?" Cam asks as she takes a sip of her cola and picks a rock off the ground, dusting off the specs of dirt on its surface.

"What are you? A child?" I laugh.

"You know you want to." She smirks, holding the rock out for me to grab.

"Fine." I roll my eyes, taking the rock from her hand and skipping it across the water.

"Beat that!" I turn to look at her, only to see that she's filming me.

"Cam!" I squeal, covering my face. She bursts out in laughter as she chases me down the pier. It doesn't take long for us to run out of breath and collapse on to the wooden floor of the pier. I rest my head next to hers with our feet sticking out in opposite directions. It's moments like these that make me forget everything bad I have going on. If there's one good thing about Cam, it's that she's the best at distracting.

The loud honk of a car's horn pulls me out of my thoughts. I realize that I'm now lying on the ground of the pier, staring up at the sky. I stand up, dusting off my jeans and wiping away the tears brimming my eyes before they can fall. It's still hard to believe that Cam is actually gone . . . that she is no longer just a call away.

Upon arriving home, I find a note on the counter in my mother's handwriting, notifying me that she and my father have left for their trip and that they will be back on Sunday.

Seeing as I only have an hour or so until the girls come over, I decide to tidy up the house and set out all of the food and snacks while I take the time to make myself look somewhat presentable.

It's weird doing things like this again. I'm so used to only doing these things with Cam that it feels foreign to be planning it with people who aren't her, but if I want to go back to who I was before and if I want to get over what happened, this is where I'm going to start. I know this isn't going to be easy—nothing about this has been easy—but when is life ever easy? My phone chimes and I look to see a message from Alison telling me that they are on their way.

After fixing my hair and changing into something cuter than what I have on, I rush downstairs and start to decorate the living room with various pillows and blankets. The pizza I ordered isn't here yet, so I put out whatever I have in my pantry, hoping it will hold us over until everything arrives. A couple of minutes later, the sound of the doorbell reverberates through the house. From the giggles coming from outside, I know it isn't the food.

"Hey—" I start but stop mid-sentence as I see that not only is Alison and Madison standing at my door, but it looks like they took it upon themselves to invite dumb and dumber.

"Are you guys serious?" I exclaim. "I told you guys not to invite them."

"Now, now, Alexa. Is that any way to treat your family?" my cousin Caleb scolds as he wraps his arm around my shoulder.

"You guys are so not coming in."

"Come on, Alexa. It'll be fun having them around!" Madison begs.

"Yeah, it'll be fun!" Braden adds in.

"I don't have a choice, do I?" I say defeatedly.

I can see how this is going to go, and it's obvious that I'm not going to get my way even though this is my house.

"Nope!" they all say at the same time, pushing past me and leaving me by the door. I close it with a sigh and follow them into the living room where they immediately start to raid my collection of movies and games that I haven't played in years. I don't think there's going to be anything fun about this at first, but half an hour later, I find myself laughing the hardest I've ever laughed in weeks as I watch them play Just Dance. I start to realize why Caleb and Braden never dance.

"You guys suck at this!" I shout over the music.

"Oh yeah? Like you can do any better," Braden shouts, not once looking away from the game.

"I know I can," I state.

"I think we know how this is going to be settled . . ." Alison pauses dramatically. "Dance battle!" she screams.

"Not happening," I say.

"Scared you're going to lose?" Caleb challenges.

Before I can reply, the doorbell rings, creating the perfect excuse.

"Oh, won't you look at that?" I say as I get up from my spot on the couch. "Looks like the food is here."

"This is so not over!" the boys shout at me. I shake my head and laugh as I open the door, preparing myself to greet the person on the other side. When I open the door, I fight the urge to shut it close again because, standing there, leaning against the wall, is Blake.

I gulp.

"Some party, huh?" he says.

CHAPTER SEVENTEEN

You know that feeling you get when you've been caught doing something wrong? That's how I feel under Blake's scrutinizing gaze, only I know I've done nothing wrong. So why does it feel that way?

"Are you going to stand there all day, or are you going to let me in?" Blake questions.

I don't realize I have just been standing here, completely zoned out for the last minute.

"Oh, uh . . . sure," I mumble, fumbling with the door. A rush of embarrassment is turning my cheeks a light tinge of pink. I step aside, letting Blake in, and I close the door behind him.

He greets my cousins and his sisters before sitting down on the couch opposite me to watch the heated dance battle between Braden and Alison. I look at Madison with a what-do-I-do expression to which she just shrugs. I successfully manage to get through an hour of Blake's company without any awkward conversation. Having the girls and my cousins here really make it impossible for Blake and I to be alone, which I'm grateful for.

After Braden and Alison finish their ultimate dance battle, which we have been watching this entire time because they keep requesting rematches, we finally decide to watch a movie. I take it upon myself to make some popcorn, given that I am the host of this very secluded get-together. The food arrived shortly after Blake did, so I make sure to set up everything on the counter while the popcorn pops. I lean against the counter while waiting for the microwave to beep as the pop of every kernel resonates throughout the kitchen.

"Hey," a deep voice says behind me, and I immediately know who it is. I have been dreading this moment the whole night, but I guess it is inevitable. Not wanting to go through this right now, I choose to do what any childish person would—ignore him.

"Alexa," he calls out again. I keep up my ridiculous act while I pour the popcorn into separate bowls. When I turn around, the bowls are snatched out of my hands and then placed on the kitchen island.

"We need to talk." He sighs apologetically at his sudden actions.

"About what?" I play dumb again, hoping this time will play out better than the day at the pier. He doesn't buy my feigned obliviousness and, instead, steps closer to me, making me take a step back.

"When are you going to stop acting like that kiss never happened?" he asks desperately. His eyes hold such frustration, and I will be lying if I say I don't feel guilty for being the reason for it. The truth is, I like Blake and really want to get to know him, but I'm no good for him. I have problems that I still need to deal with, and Blake doesn't deserve to have to deal with those things as well.

"I'll stop when you stop acting like it meant something," I reply.

My voice is serious and monotonous. I swear I can feel my heart crack at the look on Blake's face as those words leave my mouth. He doesn't reply and he nods instead.

"Thanks for making it clear," he mumbles before turning on his heel and walking out of the kitchen.

I decide not to go after him. The sound of the door lightly slamming shut is enough to make me crack. I hate the fact that I'm like this and the fact that I ruin everything I touch. The one guy I like now hates me. Blake Harper hates me, and it's no one's fault but my own.

The sound of laughter from the living room is the only thing that pulls me from my thoughts. I take a second to get myself together before plastering a smile on my face and carrying the popcorn out with me.

There's a big difference in the atmosphere here from the tension between Blake and I in the kitchen, and it seems that no one has noticed his absence or maybe they did and decided to just not say anything about it, which I'm thankful for. The thought of Blake and what just happened between us moments ago makes a knot form in my stomach. As I set the popcorn down and join everyone to watch the movie, I hope for the best. We're only into the middle of the movie when my cousins announce that they have to go after getting a phone call from my aunt, then it's just the three of us—Alison, Madison, and me. I leave the girls in the living room while I clean up the kitchen, throwing away any food wrappers and storing all the leftovers. Once everything is tidy and clean, I walk back into the living room.

"So how about we watch—"

"We need to talk," they cut me off.

"About what?" I question, feeling a sudden sense of déjà vu.

"Our brother," Alison replies and the knot in my stomach becomes tighter.

"What's there to talk about?" I question, wanting to talk about anything but Blake.

"Well, for starters, we're not going to act like we didn't notice him storm out of the house earlier," Madison says. "What's going on with you guys?"

"Nothing. I just said something that I shouldn't have, and now, I've probably made things a whole lot more complicated." I honestly don't know how to explain everything to them. I can't even explain it to myself. How can a boy I haven't even known for that long just make me question myself like this?

"Alexa, Blake likes you, like, really likes you. We're all for the idea of you two getting to know each other, but we don't want you stringing him along if you don't feel the same way," Madison says.

"So if you have no intention of letting whatever is going on between you guys happen, then you need to tell him that," Alison adds.

I want to believe that there's nothing between Blake and I, but even I know I can't trick myself into believing that. I so desperately want to just sit back and let things happen, but I'm scared—scared of getting attached to someone only to have them ripped from my life like Cam. I don't want to trust anyone with my newly mended heart only to have them break it to pieces again.

CHAPTER EIGHTEEN

For the first time in a while, things feel like they're looking up. My grades are finally back to how they used to be before everything happened, and no one at school looks at me like a puppy kicked to the curb. It's as if I'm old news, which I'm not complaining about, but what is most exciting is that my guidance counselor believes that if I stay on track, I will have a shot at getting into my dream school—New York University.

I quickly walk into the school building, trying to escape the cold. It's December now, which means that winter will be approaching soon; hence the cold weather. It also apparently means that our school's winter formal is coming up. There are banners and posters everywhere, and I watch as groups of kids hang up more.

"Aren't you excited?" Alison asks as she and Madison approach and stare at the banners in awe.

"It's going to be so much fun looking for the perfect dress," Madison adds.

Under normal circumstances, I would have been ecstatic about the dance. It's something I always look forward to, but this year, it doesn't seem all that appealing, and I know it has to do with Cam not being able to go with me.

"I don't think I'm going to go," I say. Their excitement evidently begins to fade.

"Alexa, this is the last year you're ever going to be able to go," Madison says. "You can't miss out on it."

"I don't know, guys. I don't think I'm going to be up for the glitz and glamour." I make my way to my locker with the girls following closely behind.

"Look, I know this hasn't been the best year for you, and I know you've been trying to adjust but you need to start living your life again," Alison says solemnly.

They're right. I do need to start living my life again, but it doesn't feel right without Cam.

"Alexa, please." They both give me puppy dog eyes and I smile.

"I'm only going to go for you, guys," I give in.

"Yes!" they squeal in unison.

"If you ditch me for boys, I will never forgive you, guys," I joke.

"We won't!" Alison says.

"And I'm not wearing heels."

They stop their squealing at that. Before they can protest, the bell rings, signaling the start of classes. As I head to my first class of the day, I think about what I just agreed to. The winter formal is something Cam and I have always attended together; each year was always a different experience.

But this year, I'm not really looking forward to anything much except for graduation. I only agreed to go so easily because of Alison and Madison. They've been such great friends to me these past few months, and it's the least I can do for all they've done.

The following days go by quickly, and soon, it's the end of the week. Saturday morning, I step outside to check the mail when the girls pull into my driveway and honk the horn.

"We're going shopping!" they scream excitedly and I roll my eyes.

"Now? Seriously?" I question.

"Hurry up, you have five minutes to get changed!" Madison yells.

I groan and enter my house, running up to my room and throwing on my favorite pair of jeans and a knitted sweater. Grabbing my wallet, my phone, and my keys, I run back downstairs and send a quick text to my parents to notify them that I'm heading out since they aren't home.

"Took you long enough," Madison says as she smiles at me from the front seat of the car.

"Well, thank you, guys, for showing up completely unannounced," I reply while clipping in my seatbelt. "Where are we going anyway?" I ask, though I have an idea.

"Dress shopping!" Alison says excitedly.

"Oh boy," I groan slumping into my seat.

For the next two hours, I watch the girls try on loads of dresses while I play games on my phone.

"Alexa!" Alison yanks my phone out of my hands. "Come on, you need to find a dress!"

"Fine." I sigh while sluggishly standing from the ottoman and following her to the racks of dresses.

"How about this one?" She pulls out a royal blue dress with a bedazzled bust, and I have to fight the urge to cringe.

"No," I immediately say.

She laughs at my reaction and continues to flip through the racks until her eyes land on a dress.

"This one," she states handing me the dress. I extend the dress in front of me, immediately liking the gown. It's a simple black satin dress; it's strapless, fitted at the top, and fanning out from the waist. It's perfect for me.

"I like it." I grin, taking the gown with me into the dressing room. It takes a few minutes to get into it, but once I manage to get it on, I admire myself in the mirror. It's been a while since I wore such an elegant dress, and I've forgotten how much I enjoy dressing up. I step out of the room, shoving the curtain out of the way and standing in front of the girls. Their jaws drop to the floor as they see me. I smile down at the dress, suddenly kind of excited for this dance.

We check out right away and the girls insist on paying for my dress, but I politely decline.

I swipe my card before Alison does while the clerk covers my dress in the plastic encasing. We all step out of the boutique with our dresses in hand as we decide to head home, agreeing to leave shoe shopping for tomorrow, although I already know which shoes I'm going to wear. We arrive at my house and the girls decide to stay over. We spend the night searching for makeup looks and hairstyles for the dance, and I feel like I'm slowly turning into my old self again.

The next day is rather eventful. After going out to this small cafe for breakfast, we decide to head to DSW to shop for the shoes portion of the winter formal ensemble. So far we've been here for almost two hours with the girls having no luck of finding the perfect pair of heels.

"This is hopeless!" Madison exclaims as she puts back the heels she just tried on.

"I thought that one was pretty cute," I suggest.

"That's the problem, it's cute. I need something that screams sexy," she replies.

"How are you so calm about all of this? I haven't seen you try on anything yet." Alison groans as she puts back what has to be the thirtieth pair of heels.

"I told you guys that I am not wearing heels to that thing." I scan the racks of shoes when my eyes land on a pair that will go perfectly with their dresses.

"How about these?" I hold out the heels to them and watch as they each try on a pair.

"Alexa, these are perfect!" They marvel at themselves in the mirror. I smile as a feeling of accomplishment washes over me.

"They're simple but they definitely scream sexy," Alison comments and Madison nods in agreement.

"Well, looks like we've finally found the perfect heels." They call over an employee to box up the shoes and make sure it's the right size. To think it only took two hours to find them.

CHAPTER NINETEEN

The dance is tomorrow yet, somehow, I'm not stressing about it. For the first time in a while, I'm looking forward to a fun night with my friends. It's still going to be hard, considering my best friend isn't here to take part in this tradition we've started since we've entered high school, but everyday, I'm getting more and more used to the fact that Cam is gone. Maybe that's a good thing; she would want me to go on with my life.

I turn to my closet door where my dress hangs, which is still encased in the translucent plastic covering. My eyes travel down, and I can't help but roll them at the sight of the four-inch heels the girls forced me to buy. The shoes are gorgeous, but they definitely aren't worth me possibly breaking my neck on the dance floor.

I open my vanity drawer in search of my moisturizer only to find the unopened envelope that's been waiting to be opened for months. My mouth runs dry. A part of me wants to rip through the paper and get rid of this anxiety once and for all, but the other part of me doesn't want to open that envelope only to find that I'm to blame for my best friend's death. I quickly slam the drawer shut, moving on to the next one and finding my moisturizer. After rubbing it into my face, I change into something for bed. There's no knowing how tomorrow is going to go. With my luck, it can end either very well or very badly, there's no in between. I turn to flick my lamp off before burying myself under my covers and closing my eyes.

The next morning, I wake up to the sound of my mother barging into my room. "What time is the dance?" she questions excitedly. I guess it's been awhile since I've done something as normal as attending a dance.

"It starts at six," I reply as I sluggishly slide out of bed and walk to my bathroom with my mother following closely behind. I start to brush my teeth and wash my face while giving laconic replies to my mother's endless questions.

"Can I see your dress?" she asks.

"You'll see it when I leave for the dance." I grin at her as I shoo her out of my room, deciding to get some school work done so I don't have to worry about it for the rest of the weekend. While I'm at it, I decide to do some research on New York University seeing as I will have to start sending in my application.

As of now, their overall acceptance rate is 16 percent, which is a bit discouraging but I'm not going to let that stop me from applying. They have amazing courses in journalism, which I'm almost positive is what I want to go into as a career choice. The knock on my door makes me jump, and I roll my eyes as two dark-haired girls barge in with suitcases in hand.

"It's glam time!" they say as the looks on their faces indicate that they mean business.

"It's only three o'clock, the dance doesn't start till six," I deadpan.

"Exactly, which is why if we don't start getting ready now, we won't be ready on time," Alison replies like it's the most obvious thing in the world.

"You're joking, right? I'm pretty sure I can get ready for this thing in less than an hour."

"Not even a little bit," Alison replies. "Now, come on, we don't have all day."

They each throw open their suitcases, which contain their dresses, shoes, and a ton of makeup and accessories. I am fortunately allowed to do my own makeup and decide on a natural look, which doesn't take me more than twenty minutes. Meanwhile, the girls are still working on their eye makeup.

"I'm going downstairs to get something to drink. Do you, guys, want anything?" I ask while walking towards my door.

"Water would be great," Madison says. I nod and jog downstairs in to the kitchen to find my parents both sitting at the kitchen island. They look up and smile as they see me. I can hear my mother telling my dad about the dance tonight. I try not to roll my eyes, which is something I find myself doing a lot lately.

"So a dance, huh?" he questions as he looks at me.

"Yup," I reply.

"Who's the lucky boy?"

"There is no boy."

"What about that Blake boy?" my mother interjects. I almost drop the water bottles in my hands. I haven't had any interactions with Blake in weeks, and the only time I've ever seen him is in the hallways between classes. We would catch each other's eyes and quickly look away as if it hurt to look at each other.

"What about him?" I try to keep a neutral look on my face, hoping that I don't give anything away—not that there is anything to give away in the first place.

"Well, you guys seemed pretty close at Thanksgiving dinner, and I assumed that's who you were going to the dance with," my mom replies.

"There's nothing going on between me and Blake. I don't even consider him a friend, and if you must know, I'm going to the dance with Alison and Madison who are upstairs waiting for me." I walk out of the kitchen, not wanting to be in that awkward situation any longer.

When I'm back in my room, the girls are done with their makeup, which looks flawless.

They look up at me and motion for me to come over so we can all take a group picture together.

"Dang it! It's almost five and we haven't even started on our hair yet!" Madison panics as she rushes over to her suitcase and pulls out a curling iron.

"I think I'll just leave my hair the way it is and pin it back," I say while looking at the mirror, not really feeling the need to do much with it. I like the way my natural waves look and feel that doing a middle part and pinning it back behind my ears will be the perfect look to match my dress. Besides, it's just a formal, and since it isn't prom, it doesn't make sense to go all out.

"Alex—" they both start and I hold up a finger and cut them off.

"I agreed to go to this dance with you, guys, because I want to have fun, and I'd prefer to do that comfortably without doing some elaborate hairstyle and worrying the whole night whether it still looks good." Before they can argue this, I add, "Besides, I'd much rather help the both of you style your hair since we're running on a tight schedule."

I can care less if we are late to this dance, but I know upholding a certain image is important to them. It's funny thinking about it because my image used to be everything to me, and now, look where I am. I spend the next half an hour helping Alison and Madison with their hair. I decide to leave mine in its naturally wavy state, which actually doesn't look bad at all. Alison even goes as far as to say that my hair with my dress and makeup makes me look ethereal, and I try not to scoff. As they put on their heels, I walk over to my closet and pull out the shoebox I've kept hidden in the very back. My heart is pounding as I open the lid of the box and stare at Cam's favorite pair of Converse. They're the only physical thing I have left of her, and Mrs. Carter was happy to give them to me.

"Is that why you didn't want to wear heels?" I look over my shoulder to see the girls staring at me solemnly.

"Cam loved to wear sneakers with her dress at events like the formal," I say, remembering how she wore vans to homecoming freshman year and how we laughed all night at the looks of disgust Paige kept giving her.

"Well, I think that they go perfectly with your dress," Madison says. They both smile at me and I smile back as I carefully slip the shoes on.

"Paige will have a fit seeing me in these." I laugh and they laugh with me.

"Who cares what Paige thinks," Alison responds.

"Yeah, screw Paige!" Madison adds in enthusiastically, and I almost double over in laughter.

"Screw Paige!" we all scream.

We all jump as the door swings open and my mom sticks her head in. "What's all the noi—" She stops mid-sentence as she takes in our appearances. "Honey, quick! Get the camera!" she yells.

After what feels like hours of taking pictures, we finally arrive at the dance at exactly half past six. The gym is already packed with girls in stunning dresses and their dates. It's weird being here with the girls instead of Cam, but I have to make the best out of tonight; I'm going to make the best out of tonight. Just as I expected, Paige struts up to us with a snarl on her face.

"Wow, Parker." She widens her eyes. "I was not expecting you to show, let alone show up in some beaten-up Converse." I don't take offense to her insult. I know what these shoes mean to me, and last time I checked, I don't care what Paige thinks.

"Thank you, Paige." I flash her a fake smile. "I like your dress, it really compliments your trashy personality." She scoffs before strutting off in the other direction. The girls laugh as we all high five.

"Alexa, we have to dance!" Madison begs as Queen begins to blast through the speakers.

Everyone sings along to "Don't Stop Me Now", knowing every word since it's such a classic.

After a couple of songs, we decide to take a break and find a table.

"Mind if we have a seat?" I turn my attention towards the two pests that are my cousins.

"Caleb, Braden. How did you even get into this dance? You guys don't even go here," I question, ignoring the girls as they gush over them. They, no doubt, told my cousins about this dance.

"Let's just say we finessed the system." Braden smirks, sending a wink to Alison and making her blush a bright pink.

"Shall we dance?" Caleb asks Madison, linking their arms to which she eagerly nods. My heart warms up at how cute they look together. I have a love-hate relationship with the two idiots that are Caleb and Braden, but the girls are my closest friends and they look happy.

"Alexa, aren't you coming?" Madison calls back to me.

"My feet are tired. Maybe in a bit." I want to mention our 'no boys' rule but I decide against it, wanting them to have a good time. They don't reply as the four make their way on to the dance floor, once again disappearing into the huge mass of wild students.

"Hey, you," a familiar voice calls from beside me. I turn to meet his eyes, instantly feeling a knot form in my stomach.

"What do you want, Matt?" I ask him, not in the mood to talk to him now or ever. We used to be friends, but when he and Cam went through a nasty breakup, I stopped talking to him. Now, looking at him just reminds me of her.

"I just want to talk," he calmly replies. "I didn't think you'd show up."

"Well, you thought wrong." I roll my eyes. "And that's enough talking for tonight and every day after." I stand from my chair and begin to make my way towards the girls before Matt yanks me back.

"When are you going to talk to me again?" he whines. "I messed up with Cam, I know, bu—"

"What you did to her was sick!" I raise my voice. "When I told you I never wanted to see you again, I meant it, Matt, so stay away from me!" I rip my arm out of his grasp and rush over to the refreshments table.

I take a sip of my punch and immediately spit it out. Of course, it's been spiked. This has got to be the most cliché thing to ever happen at a school dance. I clutch on to my purse and make my way out of the gym and into the hallways where the vending machines are. I punch in the numbers for a bottle of water, but the stupid dollar just won't go in. I huff in frustration and hear a chuckle behind me.

"Here, let me help you," the blond says, and I have to admit . . . he's pretty cute. He's the poster child for blond hair and blue eyes, and I try to remember where I've seen him before. He looks up at me with a water bottle in hand. I can feel my face heating up for staring at him like that.

"Thanks," I say in appreciation.

"Alexa, right?" he asks. A feeling of dread settles in my stomach at what he's probably heard about me.

"Yup, that's me," I mumble.

"I'm Evan. Evan Pratt."

"Nice to meet you, Evan Pratt." He gives me a smile that can probably blind the sun. I stand there awkwardly, not really sure of what to say or do.

"Would you like to dance, Alexa?" I'm taken aback by his proposition and step back a little.

"I would love to but my friends and I have a 'no boys' rule. Speaking of friends, I should probably get back to them," I say quickly. I wonder if he's used to girls rejecting a dance proposal from him.

With his looks, probably not, but he doesn't look fazed as he watches me speed walk to the gym doors.

"Thanks for the help." I hold up the water bottle before pushing open the doors and throwing myself back into the crowd of teenagers dancing to an upbeat song. I find the girls with my cousins by the food table and roll my eyes at how Madison laughs while Caleb stuffs his face with food.

"Hey, where'd you go?" she questions in between giggles. I look back at the gym doors to see Evan near the entrance talking to a group of boys. Alison and Madison follow my line of sight and they furrow their brows.

"Why are you staring at Evan Pratt?" they ask in unison.

"Because Evan Pratt just asked me to dance with him a few minutes ago," I reply as I bring my full attention back to them.

"Then why aren't you dancing with him?" Alison asks with an incredulous look on her face. Whoever this Evan Pratt is, he seems to be a hotshot around our school.

"Because I actually chose to honor our 'no boys' rule." Instead of responding, Alison sips from her glass of punch. "Make sure they don't drink too much," I warn Braden and Caleb, narrowing my eyes at the two of them.

"Alexa, have we ever let you down?" Caleb asks rhetorically.

"Several times," I deadpan and they roll their eyes.

Two hours later, my phone buzzes with a notification. That's when I notice it's almost eleven. Where did the time go?

I remember Mrs. Harper telling the girls that they have to be back half after eleven, and I definitely did not want them to get in trouble. She's a sweet lady, don't get me wrong, but she's frightening when she has to be. I push my way through the crowd and, after a few minutes, I finally find them next to the punch bowl. I groan, knowing those two idiots did not keep their word.

"What did I say?" I scold the two boys while flicking the both of them on their heads.

"We told them not to drink too much," Braden defends. "But we left to go to the bathroom after dancing for a bit and came back and found them here."

"Their mom is going to kill them!" I panic. "We have to go. They have to be home in twenty minutes."

They nod. Caleb takes the cups out of their hands before picking Madison up bridal style.

"Is that really necessary?" Braden rolls his eyes.

"Well, if you haven't noticed, they're heavily intoxicated and can't walk right now," Caleb replies.

Braden shakes his head before picking up Alison the same way and following me to the exit. I start the car and make my way to my house, deciding to keep the girls with me tonight and make up a story for Mrs. Harper later.

I'm grateful that my house is empty because I doubt my parents would have been happy if I show up with the girls in this state. The guys carry them up to my room and set them on my bed. Just as I'm about to change them out of their clothes, Alison sits up abruptly and regurgitates all the red punch on to my bedroom floor. Braden enters my room and his eyes focus on the puddle of vomit before turning to Alison and then to me.

"I'll get paper towels!" He runs back downstairs. I can hear him telling Caleb about what just happened. Not even a minute after, Madison runs into my bathroom, letting out everything she drank tonight as well.

The guys rush in with rolls of paper towels and every cleaning solution we own in their arms. As Caleb goes after Madison and Braden comforts Alison, I begin to clean the stain that's beginning to sink into my floor while trying not to gag. A ring begins to sound through the room and I notice it's Madison's phone. I reach for it and answer the phone, not caring to check the caller.

"Where the heck are you guys?" Blake yells through the phone. My heart suddenly begins to pound, and I struggle to muster up the courage to answer.

"Blake, the girls are with me," I finally manage to say.

"Alexa? They were supposed to be home half an hour ago."

"I know but they . . . uh . . ." I debate whether or not to lie. "They drank a little too much and won't stop throwing up."

"You've got to be kidding me," he snaps. "How irresponsible can you be?"

"Excuse me? I wasn't aware that I was a babysitter!" I raise my voice at him, not liking his attitude when I'm only trying to help to clean up the mess his sisters made, both literally and metaphorically. Before I can say anything else, the call ends and I groan as I toss the phone onto my bed.

I watch Braden pat Alison's back as she vomits into the trash bin while Caleb hands Madison a glass of water and some bread rolls.

"We are totally winning brownie points for this!" Caleb whispers to Braden as they fist bump each other.

After changing out of my dress and sending the guys home, I take all the supplies back to the kitchen and serve myself a glass of water to settle my nerves before the doorbell sounds through the house. I open it, expecting to see one of the guys but, instead, I'm met with Blake's burning green eyes.

To say that it's a shock seeing Blake, in all his glory, is an understatement. After weeks of avoiding him, I don't know what to say. It's as if I lost my voice, and I just stand there, hoping that I don't look how I feel.

"Where are they?" he demands, and I step aside to let him in. I don't say a word as I lead him upstairs and into my room where I left the girls only to walk in on Alison emptying her stomach on to my floor for the second time.

"Damn it!" I hear Blake mutter under his breath, which is less vulgar than what I feel like saying.

"Help me guide them to the bathroom," I say, not wanting another repeat of what just happened.

"I am never drinking punch again." Alison groans as she grabs the trash can and holds it close to her. I grab a pair of gloves, a bottle of cleaning spray, and the roll of paper towel before blowing a strand of hair out of my face and preparing myself for round two. Blake wordlessly kneels down beside me and starts to help clean this mess. When I agreed to go to the dance, I totally didn't expect to be cleaning up vomit by the end of it. Especially not with Blake.

"Bet this isn't your idea of a Saturday night, huh?" I say, trying to break the silence.

"Sorry for yelling at you on the phone earlier. I know this isn't your fault," he says apologetically.

"I get it. They're your sisters and their safety means everything to you." I hand him more paper towels and, together, we finally finish cleaning. I go over the spot where the vomit was, just to be sure I don't miss a spot.

"Is it okay if they stay with you for the night?" he asks me. "Our mom will freak if they're hungover in the morning and it'd be best she doesn't see them like this."

"Of course. It's no problem," I say without hesitation.

"Don't worry about explaining either. I've got it covered," he reassures me.

"Thank you." I give him a small smile before turning towards my bathroom where Alison's groans are finally starting to cease.

"I should probably get going," he says.

"I'll walk you out." I follow him down the stairs and, just as he's about to open the door, he stops and turns back to me.

"Alexa?" he says with his eyes focused on mine.

"Yeah?"

He's about to say something before a look of hesitation crosses his face and he seems to think better of it.

"Goodnight," he says instead as he steps through the door and into the night. I yell out a goodnight as he gets into his car and pulls out of my driveway. *Well, that went way better than I thought it would.*

I head upstairs and make sure Alison and Madison are comfortable in my bed before setting out some clothes for them to change into in the morning. Changing them out of their dresses is something I would rather not do right now. I collapse on to the bed in the guest room and replay tonight's events in my head. My cousins crashing the party, the girls ditching me for said cousins and then the girls getting drunk off the stupid punch even though I told those idiots not to let them drink too much. And there's Blake . . . and then there's Evan Pratt. The mysterious blue-eyed blond who everyone seems to know about except for me. Even his name sounds like something out of a movie.

CHAPTER TWENTY

December is quickly coming to an end, and it's nearing the time to take midterms before we're off for winter break. I'm sitting in a secluded area of our school's library with Alison and Madison as we all study for our exams. Well, I'm studying while Alison and Madison talk about their plans for winter break.

"Sleepovers are a must," Madison starts as I continue to read the study guide that Mr. Bronson, my physics teacher, gave to our class, which, by the way, is no help. How the heck am I supposed to remember the formula for buoyancy when I can't even remember basic math formulas?

"We should also have cute lunch dates and—" Suddenly, she stops talking mid-sentence. I look up at her to see what's caught her attention.

"Don't look . . ." Alison starts. "But I'm pretty sure Evan Pratt is walking over here."

Even though she told me not to look, I look anyway just as he arrives at our table. There he is, standing in front of me, with his blue eyes sparkling and the sunlight filtering through the library windows making his golden-blond hair illuminate like an ember in the ashes.

"Hey," he says as his confident demeanor suddenly turns into an awkward, shy one.

"Hey?" I say back, clearly confused as to why he's here. Before he's able to say anything, Alison cuts through the tension.

"I think we lost something somewhere." She smirks at me.

"Y-yeah, we're going to go find it." Madison stands from her seat as well, joining her sister as they walk to the other side of the library.

"Well, they're slick." He turns to me with a small smirk on his face. I fight the urge to roll my eyes at how ridiculous the girls are.

"So can I help you?" I ask, looking directly into his eyes, which must not be something he's used to because a look of surprise flashes across his face. If he's the type of boy the girls says he is, then he must be used to girls not being able to look him in the eyes.

"Actually, I came over here because we didn't really get to know each other much at the dance, and I wanted to invite you to come watch my lacrosse practice today."

"You want me to watch you practice?" I ask incredulously.

"Yeah?" he replies in the form of a question. "Well, n-no, not really, more like hangout there and we could get some food after?" I stifle a laugh at how nervous he's acting.

Nervousness is something I would've thought is foreign to him, especially when talking to girls but apparently not.

"I'm sorry, but I've just been really busy lately. I don't think I have the time," I say apologetically.

I look at the girls who are not so discreetly hiding behind a bookshelf and ignore the what-are-you-doing looks they're giving me.

"No problem," he replies coolly. "How about you come and watch the game tomorrow instead?"

"If I can fit that into my schedule, you may or may not see me there." I smirk at him and he lets out a laugh while running his hands through his golden locks.

"Alright, then I guess I may or may not see you tomorrow." He winks at me before walking away and the girls immediately come running over with furious looks on their faces.

"What the heck, Alexa! You know damn well that you're not busy tomorrow!" Alison exclaims.

"How could you pass up the opportunity to watch Evan Pratt practice?" Madison screams.

"Since you guys seem to like him so much, why don't you go watch him practice instead?" I joke.

"Because Evan Pratt is interested in you!" they answer in unison and the librarian hisses at us to be quiet.

"So you guys don't think it's weird at all how Evan Pratt, who I've never even heard of until a few days ago, has suddenly taken an interest in me?"

"Well, aren't you the least bit interested in him?" Alison questions.

"No," I reply, which isn't a total lie. I have to admit that he did have me intrigued, but I'm not interested in him in the way he seems to be interested in me.

"You know what," Madison declares, "we are going to that lacrosse game tomorrow, and you are going to come with us because Evan freaking Pratt asked you to."

"What's the big deal with Evan Pratt?" I ask. "Why is it such a big deal that I talk to him?" They both go quiet and I don't miss the look they give each other.

"Let's just go to the game, okay?" Alison says, completely avoiding my question. "It could be fun and you need a break from all this studying you've been doing." I'm not stupid. I know they're hiding something from me, but I decide that now isn't the time to ask.

"Fine," I give in. "We'll go watch the game, but you guys are buying me food after."

"Deal."

The remainder of the day consists of me attending class, going home, more studying and then going to bed just to wake up the next day and repeat it all over again. It's the same thing I've been doing every day this week, except today is different. Today, I will be going to a lacrosse game. The game itself didn't actually start till six o'clock so when I got home from school, I watched a movie with my parents and then made my way upstairs to get ready when it was over.

After looking through my closet, I opt for a pair of denim jeans and a gray knitted sweater since it's starting to get cold outside. I'm finally able to put back on all the weight that I've lost the last few months. I smile at the girl I see in the mirror. The girl I recognize from before everything happened and, though it's been hard, I'm doing better at coping with Cam's death. I have to give the girls credit for lending me their shoulders when I didn't have one to lean on and for refusing to let me let my life go to waste.

My eyes travel to the drawer where Cam's letter lay inside. I have put off reading it for way too long and I know I should just do it, but today has been such a good day and there's no guarantee that what I will find inside won't destroy me. I promise myself that I will read Cam's letter after the game. My phone dings, breaking me out of my trance; it's a text from Madison telling me that she and Alison are waiting outside. After grabbing my purse and keys, I meet them outside, greeting them as I get into their car.

"Well, somebody's in a good mood." Madison smirks at me through the mirror. "May we ask why?"

"I just feel good today." I shrug, strapping on my seatbelt.

The girls decide to stop for coffee on the way to the game, and I sip on it as we make our way to the game. Once we arrive at the field, we find a spot on the bleachers, which isn't too full, fortunately. The crowd begins to cheer as the guys run on to the field in their uniforms. I can see Evan at the start of the line with a bright smile on his face as he waves at some freshmen girls, and I swear, they almost faint. I laugh at them before my eyes lock on Blake.

I notice the uniform on his body and I curse under my breath. I can't believe I forgot that he's on the lacrosse team. For some odd reason, knowing Blake is here just makes me even more nervous than I already am. His eyes look up from his cleats to the crowd and then his eyes find mine. His face is unreadable like always, and before we can look at each other any longer, my attention is drawn to Evan who is now standing in front of me, leaning on the edge of the bleachers.

"You came." He smiles at me and I nod at him.

"Who are you guys playing against?" I ask, feeling a bit stupid for not doing my research beforehand.

"St. Andrews," he replies. "A few guys from the team and I are going out for a bite after the game. Do you, girls, want to join?" he addresses all three of us. I'm unsure of what to reply so I turn to the girls who nod quickly.

The thought of going out with guys from school makes me uncomfortable. I would much rather go home after this, but before I can object, Alison beats me to it.

"We'll be there!" she says. Evan smiles at us, clearly amused.

"You sure?" He turns to me. I sigh, knowing that I have to stop being such a downer, but then I remember Cam's letter at home waiting for me to come through on my promise and finally open it. Opening that letter means there's a chance this good day can be cut short depending on what that letter says. Maybe I should enjoy today as much as possible before opening it.

Without another thought, I look at Evan with a small smile on my face. "I'll be there."

* * *

We're two quarters into the game. Surprisingly, I'm having a great time. Our school is annihilating St. Andrews, and I can't help but feel bad for the members of their team. Evan looks up at me from the field with a cheeky grin on his face and I smile back. Blake comes into view from behind him and my smile falters at the way he's looking at me. Once the whistle blows for halftime, I decide to head to the concession stand to get some snacks for me and the girls. As I stand in line, I look up at the menu, suddenly craving a milkshake. There are three people in front of me, and just as the line moves up one, I'm tugged from behind the corner into a tall, hard body.

I stop myself from screaming as I recognize who pulled me out of the line.

"I was about to get a milkshake!" I whine at Blake who still holds the same expression on his face from earlier.

"Evan Pratt? Really?" He gives me an incredulous look, and it takes me a minute to understand what he means.

"That's none of your business," I say.

"Alexa, you can't be serious."

"Look, there's nothing going on between us, okay? I didn't even want to come," I say, confused as to why I'm trying to prove myself to him.

What's even more confusing is how I can't help but think about how good he looks in his uniform and how much I want to run my hands through his hair. The whistle blows and I notice that people are starting to head back to the bleachers for the second half of the game, and the teams are getting ready to go back onto the field.

"I don't understand you," he whispers quietly before letting go of my arm, which I don't even realize he was holding on to till now.

He gives me one last look before running back to the field. I step out from around the corner, seeing everyone has now made their way back to the bleachers and the game has started again.

"You and me both," I whisper as I watch Blake catch the ball and sprint down the field. I head back to my spot on the bleachers, suddenly not feeling in the mood for a shake anymore.

"Where are the snacks?" the girls question once they see me empty-handed.

"They're all out of food," I lie, faking an annoyed expression.

They both shrug before joining the crowd and cheering wildly for Blake who has just scored another one of his many goals. My eyes linger on him as I try to suppress all the emotions that suddenly appear when I think about him. *He deserves better*, I remind myself, not even paying attention to the game anymore or to Evan Pratt who watches me from afar.

* * *

"Who knew lacrosse was so intense!" Alison exclaims, throwing her hands up.

"Bet you're happy you came, huh?" Madison elbows me, and I smile while shaking my head at them.

The game has just ended and our school won by nine goals, which isn't a surprise. Now, we're waiting by the parking lot where Evan told us to meet him and the guys.

"Why didn't you guys tell me that Blake was playing?" I ask.

"We thought you knew he played lacrosse," Alison replies.

"I did. I guess I just forgot." I wrap my arms around myself as a cold wind passes by.

"Cold?" Evan says out of nowhere, catching me by surprise as he places his jacket over my shoulders. It has his name in small font on the upper right side and the lacrosse symbol under it. His jacket immediately warms me up, but it just doesn't feel right wearing it.

"Thanks." I smile, not wanting to be rude by declining the sweet gesture.

Three boys, who I recognize from the field, join us. "So this is the infamous Alexa you can't stop talking about," one of them says. He looks at Evan's jacket sitting on my shoulders and I look at Evan to see a tint of red on his cheeks. I skim over the rest of the guys and don't miss the way one is looking at Alison who becomes shy under his gaze.

"Where's Blake? I thought he was coming." Evan breaks the silence and I become anxious at the mention of Blake's name. *Great, this night can't get any worse.*

"I'm right here," Blake says as he suddenly appears and joins our group. *Yup, things have just gotten worse.* He looks at me briefly and I look down at my shoes, avoiding his gaze.

"Was starting to think you bailed on us," Evan replies and Blake laughs.

"And leave you guys alone with my sisters?" I look at the girls who were quiet up until now.

They playfully shove Blake, which doesn't have much effect on him because of how tall he is. A smile unknowingly forms on my face as I watch him ruffle their hair and at how he looks at them with so much love in his eyes. I follow the girls to their car as we all agree to meet at a diner close by.

"Looks like things between you and Evan are heating up," Madison says from the passenger seat as she motions to Evan's jacket.

"I'm not interested and you, guys, know that."

"You say that now," Alison chimes in as she makes a right turn, following Evan's car as he leads.

"Don't think I didn't notice the way you and that guy were looking at each other," I accuse and she immediately shuts up.

"I thought you were involved with one of my cousins anyway."

"Braden's nice and all but we're just friends," she starts. "Besides, things are heating up with Caleb and Madison, and if they get married wouldn't that make Braden and I brother- and sister-in-law?" We all laugh at that. I smile at the thought of Caleb and Madison being together.

We finally pull up to a small diner that looks a lot like the ones you see in movies or shows. I wonder why I've never been here before. We step into the joint and walk towards the far corner where the guys have already slid into a booth. I didn't notice that the girls are already seated until Alison yanks me into the booth next to her. Luckily, I'm seated at the end, which means I can easily get in and out in case anything happens. The waitress comes up and takes our drink orders before asking how the checks will be divided.

"We'll all be paying separately, but you can put the girls on mine," Evan says. My eyes widen and I rapidly shake my head at him.

"I can pay for my own food," I say.

"I insist." He nods at me assuredly and I sink back into the booth, not having the energy to argue this. After taking everyone's orders, the waitress walks off.

I look in front of me where Evan is sitting, suddenly growing uncomfortable. Going out isn't exactly my thing, let alone with a guy who's interest in me isn't so easily reciprocated. Alison has already sparked conversation with that one guy who I have learned is named Noah. I smile as she giggles at something he says into her ear; I'm happy for her. Madison sits next to Blake, clearly unfazed by the guys as they try flirting with her. Blake's attention is glued to his phone screen, and I grow a bit curious as to what it is that has him so focused.

"So . . ." Evan breaks the silence between us. "What did you think of the game?"

"It was fun," I admit. "I never knew lacrosse could be so intense." He laughs at my confession and I force a smile.

The waitress returns with our drinks and tells us our food will be out shortly. Everyone ordered burgers while I decided on waffles, which definitely isn't just breakfast food. My eyes shoot up towards the door at the sound of the bells ringing to signify some has walked in. A girl steps in, covering her head with a jacket, and for some reason, I smile. Maybe it's her laugh that seems to lighten up the mood or the fact that she seems happy even though she's soaked from head to toe because of the rain. It kind of reminds me of Cam. My smile vanishes quickly as a guy runs through the door, meeting the girl. Flashbacks and memories suddenly begin coming back at the sight of the guy I haven't seen since his sister's funeral . . . since Cam's funeral.

It's as if I've done something to draw his attention towards me because when his eyes meet mine, he recognizes me instantly. His eyes scan the area around me, examining everyone I'm with. I don't fail to notice the hint of anger in his eyes and the way his nostrils flare to signal that he's angry; Cam was just like him. I begin to feel sick to my stomach and I turn away from his gaze, excusing myself from the group and making my way towards the restroom. I push the swinging door open and use my arms to hold myself over the sink. I stare at myself in the mirror, seeing how pale I've gotten in the last minute. I turn the knob on the sink and splash some cold water on my face, hoping to bring back some color.

There are several thoughts swarming my mind, but the one that is bugging me the most is, why is he back in town? I dry my face and tie my hair up into a ponytail before gaining the courage to leave the restroom. Just as I'm about to round the corner, I collide with a body coming from the opposite direction. The person's arms grip my arms to keep me from falling, and once I've steadied, I manage to see who it is and my previous anxiety returns.

"Zach," I breathe out. "W-what are you doing here?"

"I can ask you the same question," he snaps at me. "Seems like you've moved on fairly quickly."

"Zach, what are you talking about?" It's like he's angry at me when he has no right to be.

"So you're telling me that you're not here hanging out with your new friends?"

"No, but I'm no–"

"That's what I thought."

"Zach, calm down! You have no right to come at me like this. What'd you expect? That I'd live my life grieving and never moving on from this? Don't try to make it seem like I forgot about her. I loved her more than I love myself!" I snap back at him, my heart pounding faster and tears brimming my eyes. I'm not surprised that he's acting like this though. Cam's death has affected him so much. She was his best friend too.

"Have you read the letter?" My heart stops at his question. *How did he know about it? Did he read it?*

"How do you know about it?" I ask.

"Alexa, I'm the one who found it." He lets out a breath.

"I haven't read it," I reply. "I was planning to read it tonight." He nods at me and stands there in what seems like deep thought.

"She wrote that letter before she died. She knew what she was going to do," he mumbles more to himself than to me and my eyebrows knit together.

"Zach, did you read the letter?" My voice is shaky as I ask.

"No," he says. "I would never invade Cam's privacy like that, especially since the letter was addressed to you. But, if there's anything in there I should know, you tell me. Okay?" The pleading in his eyes breaks my heart and I nod at him.

"Take care of yourself, Alexa." He walks back into the dining area, leaving me confused and worried about what can possibly be in that letter.

I still don't understand why Zach is even in town in the first place. After Cam's death, he moved away to another city and started college. He was always so close to Cam when she was alive, and I guess maybe that's why he blamed himself the most for her death. He didn't notice what she was going through. Then again, neither did I. I can still remember how heartbroken he was to see his sister's lifeless body in that casket the day of her funeral. We all suffered from her death, but Zach was different. For Zach, it was like he lost a piece of himself. Yes, Cam was like a sister to me, but that will never compare to the mourning of her real brother. It isn't shocking to see that this tragedy has left him so defensive and angry. It left all of us that way.

"Alexa, are you okay?" I'm snapped out of my trance by that deep voice I know so well. I shake my head to rid my thoughts before turning to Blake.

"Y-yeah." I nod. "I just got a phone call."

"Well, the orders are here." He points back to the tables as he makes his way to the men's restroom.

"Right," I say. "Thanks."

"By the way," he calls out to me again, "your phone started ringing back at the table."

I nod at him, mentally facepalming myself at my fail of a save. The corner of his lips turns up into a slight smirk before he enters the restroom completely. I walk back to the table, slightly embarrassed at the encounter.

"Is everything okay?" Evan asks, examining me as I get into the booth.

"Yeah." I feign a smile. "Everything's fine."

CHAPTER TWENTY-ONE

Every day since receiving that letter with my name written in Cam's loopy handwriting, I have put off reading it. I was scared—scared to read the contents of the letter and even more scared of the fact that her death may or may not be my fault.

In an attempt to let go and move on from Cam's death and accept the fact that she's gone and there's nothing I can do about it, I selfishly push any thoughts of that letter to the back of my mind the way Cam used to push down homework assignments she wouldn't get to till the day it was due to the bottom of her bag, but I've put it off for too long now. In some ways, I think that running into Zach tonight has been a push from Cam to suck it up and just read it already. So tonight, I'm finally going to do it.

"Hey," Alison says from her spot in the driver's seat as she looks at me through the rearview mirror. "You okay? You've been pretty quiet since you came back from the bathroom."

"Yeah, did something happen?" Madison asks.

"I'm fine," I reply with a smile. "Just tired."

I can't tell Alison and Madison about the letter without explaining to them why I didn't tell them about it in the first place and why I've put off reading it for so long. The only person who knows about the letter is Blake, and he's the last person I should be talking to about this.

They pull into my driveway and I smile at the both of them as they look at me.

"Thanks for tonight, guys. I had a great time," I say, trying to soothe their worries about me.

"Of course," they both reply. I say my goodbyes before making my way to my door, feeling like I want to throw up as I fumble with my keys. My parents are up and snuggled up on the couch when I walk into the living room and throw my keys into the dish on the table.

"Hey, honey!" my mom calls out. "Did you have fun tonight?"

"Yeah." I smile. "I did."

"Did you eat?" my dad questions. "Your mother made Italian tonight."

"Thanks but we stopped at a diner after so I'm good for the night." Not that I will be able to stomach anything else at this point anyway.

"Okay, we'll be down here if you need anything." I nod and quickly leave, rushing up the stairs and into my bedroom.

I lean against my door once it's shut and try to catch my breath. *Maybe I should shower first and then read the letter.* Even I know that this is just another excuse for putting it off longer than I needed to, but maybe a nice shower is just what I need to calm and prepare myself for whatever I'm going to read tonight. Without a second thought, I grab my robe and a towel as I rush into my bathroom and quickly shut the door as if something were chasing me from behind.

After my shower, which did little to calm my nerves, I sigh as I stare at myself in the mirror. For starters, my body has regained most of its weight and the color has reappeared on my cheeks. It's crazy to think of how badly not only my appearance has gotten but my mental state as well. My self-esteem deteriorated and my confidence was nearly nonexistent. I had gotten to the point of being repulsed by my own reflection. I was a girl that had been hit hard by the death of her best friend—so hard that who I was partially went with her.

But now, I'm ready. I've managed to get my courage back, and I know I'm strong enough to get the rest of myself back, too, even if it takes me an eternity to do so.

I turn on the sink, letting the cold water run. I'm going to be okay; I'm going to get back up from this hard hit because if there's one thing I know, it's that when life pushes you down, you try landing on your back. Because if you can look up, you can get up, and I am looking up. I swing the bathroom door open, now determined to read whatever is written in that letter and do my best to cope with it.

I take a seat at my desk, slowly opening up the top drawer where the letter is buried. I dip my hand in, feeling around through all the miscellaneous items that litter the drawer. My fingers land on the crisp paper of the envelope. I suddenly want to flinch away and shut the drawer . . . but I don't.

I slide the envelope out and set it on the desk in front of me. My breathing has become heavier and ragged just at the sight of my name written on the front.

Okay, Alexa. You can do this. It's just like ripping off a Band-Aid.

Except this Band-Aid can make the wound a lot worse after it's ripped.

I slip the letter opener under the flap of the envelope, taking a deep breath before running it across. I pull out the tri folded piece of paper inside, holding it in both of my hands. Tons of ideas and worries begin to flood my mind of what could be written, but before I can get distracted, I unfold a third of the letter, seeing the first two words written in black ink.

Dear Alexa . . .

CHAPTER TWENTY-TWO

I don't think that things can get any worse. After all I've been through, things can't possibly get as bad as they are. I'm finally moving on from Cam's death, and things are looking up for me; things are actually getting better.

The thing about life is that it's cruel and it waits for no one. Things can be the greatest they've been in a while, but then, that happiness is suddenly ripped away from you like some violent storm destroying everything in its path. Things aren't getting better for me; they are just the calm before the actual storm hit. I sit in the parking lot of my high school with Cam's words reverberating through my mind.

Dear Alexa,
None of this is your fault.

School started hours ago but I can't bring myself to leave my car. My eyes are puffy and bloodshot from staying up for hours crying and reading Cam's letter over and over again.

You are the greatest friend that anyone could ever ask for, and I'm so lucky to have had someone like you by my side these past three years, so don't you ever think any of this was your fault.

You will think that it will get easier to read each time, but it doesn't get easier; it only gets harder. After what has to be the hundredth time reading it, I just can't read it anymore, but I remember every word she wrote. Her words are now engraved into my mind.

I just can't take it anymore. I'm tired, Alexa. Tired of feeling the way I do, and I know you're wondering why I haven't come to you with how I'm feeling. Why I've been wearing this mask of happiness when I'm far from happy. Don't blame yourself for not seeing the signs that I wasn't okay. I made sure there weren't any signs to see.

All this time, I blamed myself for Cam's death. I blamed myself for not seeing the signs, but she made sure there weren't any signs for me to see. She made sure that I couldn't see that anything was wrong, and it hurts me that she didn't come to me when she was feeling unhappy. I was her best friend and she didn't come to me.

I know I should've talked to you or anyone for that matter about what's going on. Maybe I wouldn't be writing this letter if I had, but at this point, I don't think that there's anything anyone could do to help me out of this dark place. I don't know how else to say what I'm going to tell you next so I'm just going to say it. I'm pregnant, Alexa. And it hurts so much more knowing what I am going to do after I finish writing this.

I feel like I'm going to throw up from all the nerves and Cam's revelation. My phone starts to chime, and I know it's from Alison and Madison who have been trying to reach me since this morning.

I'm not sure if I should be telling you this because I don't know what you're going to think of me after you read this. Am I a monster for doing this? Only a monster would take their life knowing they would also be taking another life, right? Monsters like me don't deserve to live.

I take a deep breath before opening my car door. I need to do this before lunch is over.

I know you're wondering who I was stupid enough to get knocked up by. I decided to give Matt another chance.

I walk through the school's front entrance, feeling like my legs would give out from beneath me.

He said he missed me. That he loved me and was ready to be the boyfriend he couldn't be our sophomore year. I was so stupid to believe him, Alexa.

The hallways are mostly empty except for a few kids walking around. They look at me and take in my frantic appearance, but I pay them no mind as I head for the cafeteria.

He hurt me. Not physically but mentally. He might as well have hit me because that's what it felt like. I went to his house to tell him when the test read positive. I didn't know what to do, but when I got there, I saw Paige sneaking out of his backyard and I just couldn't. I broke down right there in the middle of the street. A few weeks later, Matt stopped talking to me when he found out. I can't bear the thought of burdening you with all of this when things were going so well for you. I don't even want to think about how disappointed you're going to be. I can't tell my parents. Things are getting worse here and my parents would kill me. I have no one, Alexa.

My breathing gets heavier as I see the double doors leading to the cafeteria.

I can't do this anymore. There's no coming back from this. I'm tired and I just need everything to stop. You must think that this is the stupidest reason ever. That all I have to do is talk to someone and everything will be okay. You wouldn't understand. It isn't that simple. I wish it were because then, things would be different. Just know that I love you. That even if I'm not there with you, my love for you always will be. Please tell my parents and Zach that I love them.

I'm sorry,

Cam

I burst through the doors and only a few people noticed me at first. As I make my way to the center of the cafeteria, I can feel everyone's eyes start to follow. I'm aware of someone calling my name, but I cancel out everything around me as my eyes lock on Matt who laughs at something his friend told him. He sees me coming, but before he can say anything, my fist collides with his face.

"What the hell?" he yells as he gets up, holding his hand to his bleeding lip.

"It's all your fault!" I scream as I bang my fists on to his chest, not being able to stop the tears that are now spilling down my cheeks.

"What the hell are you talking about?" he screams back, trying to block my hits.

Everyone in the cafeteria is watching us in shock, but I don't care.

"Cam killed herself because of you!" An expression I can't even explain settles over Matt's face and people start to murmur. I can hear the sound of people calling my name, getting closer, but I need to do this. I need to make him hurt as much as he hurt Cam.

"She would be here if it weren't for you!" I can feel the pain in my fists as I continue to hit him, but I push that pain to the back of my mind.

"Shut the hell up!" he says. "You have no idea what you're talking about. I loved Cam. I fucking loved her and I still do, so shut the hell up!" His face is red and he looks like he's about to cry, but he doesn't, which for some reason only makes me angrier.

I pull my arm back to hit him again, but someone's arms circle around my waist, pulling me back. I struggle in their grasp as I continue to scream at Matt.

"Alexa, stop." I hear Blake whisper. I turn around to see Alison and Madison standing by his side as he holds on to me with a mixture of emotions on their faces. Just then, the doors to the cafeteria open and standing there is Mrs. Frey, our school's principal.

"You two," she says, pointing at Matt and I. "My office, now!" I shrug out of Blake's grasp and wipe my face as I walk out of the cafeteria with my head held high. Madison, Alison, and Blake follow closely behind me with Matt angrily in tow.

"You three can wait out here," she says to Blake and the girls as she motions for Matt and I to head inside her office.

She points to the two chairs across from her desk and we both sit down. I'm so angry that I don't even care that I will most likely get into trouble for this. I want Matt to pay for this. He should be the one six feet under, not Cam.

"Someone is going to explain to me what that was out there." Her voice is low yet holds a great amount of power. "Mr. Carpenter, you may start."

"W-well . . ." He turns to look at me. I wait for him to rat me out—to tell her everything. "I was in the cafeteria and Alexa walked in all angry." I take a deep breath as the principal orders him to continue.

"She was mad because . . ."

"Because?" Mrs. Frey grows impatient.

"Because I cheated on her," he lies and my eyes snap towards him, widening at his fake explanation. "So she punched me."

"Is that so?" Mrs. Frey turns to me, and I freeze in place, not knowing what to say.

I want her to know what Matt did. I want her to know what he did. I want her to see him for the monster he is, but the more I think about it, the more unsure I am if that is the right choice. Everyone will know about Cam's pregnancy. Do I really want her to be remembered that way? To be remembered as the girl who got pregnant by Matt Carpenter and killed herself? She doesn't deserve that.

"It's true," I choke out, following my brain even though my heart tells me to do the complete opposite.

"Well . . ." Mrs. Frey stands from her chair, her next words directed towards me. "It seems you had a valid reason to act that way towards Mr. Carpenter. That being said, school is not the place to handle your relationship issues, Ms. Parker. That kind of behavior is unacceptable, especially coming from a student such as yourself." I sink into my seat, hating the fact that we now have the school principal believing such a stupid lie.

"And as for you, Mr. Carpenter . . ." She looks at him, causing him to sit up in his seat. "I hope you realize that infidelity is a cowardly act, and you will apologize to Ms. Parker." He nods at her, a look of relief clear on his face.

"Now, considering Alexa did engage in physical contact by striking you, I have to enforce some kind of discipline," she says, retrieving the stack of passes and filling one of them out before ripping it off and handing it to me. "Detention." I take the slip from her, relieved. This could have been worse—should have been worse.

"And for you, Matthew, you have detention too." She gives him a stern look. "Maybe it will knock some sense into you." Matt takes the detention slip from her hands before sinking back into his seat.

"Don't let this happen again. You two are dismissed." We leave her office, and I don't say a word to Matt as he follows behind me.

"You're welcome, by the way, for saving you back there," he says. "I could have easily gotten you a suspension if I told her the truth." I want to turn around and hit him again, but my rage from the cafeteria has seemingly disappeared and is instead replaced with exhaustion. I'm too tired to do anything. My fists throb in pain now that the adrenaline has worn off, but the exhaustion and pain won't do anything to stop the hate I have for Matt from growing inside of me.

"Don't," I warn as I turn around to face him. "Don't act like you 'saving me back there' is going to make up for everything you've done." A look of hurt flashes across his face. "It's your fault she's gone," I say to dig the knife in even deeper.

"You're wrong." His voice wobbles as he clenches his fists. "I loved her."

"Then, where were you when she was pregnant and alone?" He takes a sudden intake of breath as if the air has been knocked out from his lungs. He doesn't say anything else as I give him one last look before walking into the main hallway where Alison, Madison, and Blake are waiting.

"Is everything okay?" Alison questions as she notices me walking towards them.

"Are you getting suspended?" Madison asks.

"No," I answer Madison's question. "Just a detention."

"What happened back there?" Alison asks.

The three of them look at me, expecting me to explain my actions from just minutes ago, but something's holding me back.

"I don't know." I sigh and the looks on their faces tell me that they're not letting this go.

"Come on, Alexa." Alison sighs. "We heard you tell Matt it was all his fault that Cam died."

"Why can't you just tell us the truth?" Madison pleads.

"Look, guys. It's really no big deal." I shrug them off, desperately wanting them to drop this before I break down again.

"You always say that," Alison complains. "There's clearly something happening and you won't tell us!"

"I don't want you guys to worry," I mumble, a bit taken aback by her sudden rise of voice.

"Alexa," Madison huffs. "We're your friends. It's our job to worry."

"You know what? You're right," I breathe out. "You guys deserve the truth after all you've done for me."

"We're listening." I bite on my bottom lip in thought. *I guess I'm doing this.*

"A few months ago, Cam's mom came to my house." I take a deep breath, feeling that it's suddenly becoming hard for me to talk about this. "She gave me a letter with my name on it that Cam had left behind before she died." They remain quiet as they nod, signaling me to continue.

"I kept the letter in my drawer because I was too scared to read it up until last night. Last night at the diner, I took so long in the bathroom because I saw Zach."

"Zach? As in Cam's brother Zach?" Alison questions.

"Yes." My voice begins to waver. The more I think of the information I'm about to spill, the more difficult it is to actually get the words out. "He told me he was the one who found the letter and wanted to know if I've read it yet, so when I got home, I finally built up the courage to read it."

"What did it say?" they both ask in unison.

"It said . . ." My voice is wobbly and I can feel the tears threatening to spill any second. "It said that Cam was pregnant." I can feel a single tear fall as the words leave my lips. "And that Matt was the father." There's a sharp intake of breath, and Alison's eyes gloss over as she listens to me.

"She told him and he just stopped talking to her." I leave out the details about Paige being at Matt's house and the state of Cam's home life. I begin to cry, not being able to hold back any more tears.

"Alexa . . ." Madison starts.

"And now, she's gone." I sob uncontrollably. "She's gone and it's all his fault!" I'm unable to compose any more words and I start to gasp for air.

I feel their arms around me as they try their best to comfort me, but it's no use. That letter reminds me of everything I have been trying so hard to get over these last months. Now, it's all coming back stronger than ever, and I don't think I can handle it.

"You can't stay here like this. We're taking you home," Madison says, and I'm too emotionally and physically drained to put up a fight. *I should go home.*

"We're just going to get our stuff. We'll be right back," Alison assures me. I nod before the two walk off towards their lockers, which are in the next hallway.

I have forgotten that Blake is still here until I see him in my peripheral. He's already looking at me when I turn to him with concern in his eyes. I can't imagine what I must look like right now, and I begin to grow embarrassed by the fact that he's witnessed another one of my meltdowns.

"You throw a mean punch, you know," he says suddenly. I know it's his attempt at making me feel better, which it does because I can't help but laugh. His eyes remain on mine, and I don't notice that he's gotten closer to me until he's standing right in front of me.

"Why are you looking at me like that?" I question him. I can feel my face heating up by the second, and I can only imagine how red it must be right now.

"I like seeing you laugh," he whispers. "You deserve to laugh."

"Yeah. Well, apparently, the universe does not agree with you," I reply, taking a step back to distance myself from him. It's not that I don't trust Blake; it's more so that I don't trust myself around him. "It seems like everything I love most is being ripped away from me."

"Look, Alexa—"

"What, Blake?" I sigh. "Are you going to tell me that it's going to get better? Because it won't. It never gets better. My best friend killed herself and I did nothing." I'm taken completely by surprise when Blake's arms wrap around me.

It's like Blake embracing me opens up the water faucet inside of me, and my body begins to shake as I silently cry. He doesn't pull away and, instead, hugs me tighter as he runs one of his hands through my hair.

"You're stronger than you think, Alexa. You're one of the strongest people I've ever met." We stay like that for a few minutes until my crying has ceased. I begin to pull away, but I stop when Blake's eyes meet mine.

For a minute, all I can think about is Blake and everything that's happened between us. I think about the kiss and how I rejected him when everything inside of me is telling me otherwise. How I put my feelings for him aside for what I thought was his protection. The truth is, Blake doesn't need protection. He's trying to be here for me, and I'm not letting him because I'm so scared to let someone else into my life again. I'm pushing him away when my heart wants him closer.

"Blake . . ." I whisper, scared of ruining the feeling of calm we're engulfing ourselves in.

"Yes?" he says.

"I don't want to push you away anymore," I breathe out as my eyes remain focused on his.

"Good." He nods. "Because I don't want you to push me away anymore either." Our faces are now dangerously close to each other.

Memories of Thanksgiving begin to make an appearance, and I just want to feel how I felt when I kissed Blake—happy and without a care in the world. I don't stop Blake as he begins to lean in . . . that is until I hear footsteps and I quickly push him away.

"Alright, we're ready!" I turn to the girls who are now carrying their bags and coats. "Did we miss anything?"

"Nope," Blake replies a little too quickly.

"What Blake said." I try my best to play it off. "Nothing at all."

But it isn't nothing. That moment is everything to me because in that moment, I feel like everything will be okay.

CHAPTER TWENTY-THREE

Detention is something I never thought I will experience, but then again, I've been through more in the last few months than I will have never thought I will go through in my entire lifetime.

Today is the last day before winter break. I've just finished my last midterm exam. Instead of going home like I want to, here I am sitting in detention for the next hour, which won't be that bad if I were allowed to go on my phone or do anything at all. Heck, I will even be fine with doing work if it means I don't have to sit here and watch the hands on the clock move agonizingly slow. Matt sits as far away from me as he can, which is a smart move on his part as I'm tempted to go over there and knock his teeth out. However, no matter how angry I am at him and how much I hate him at the moment, there's a small part of me that actually feels bad.

He looks awful as if he has just woken up from the dead. He glances at me and I quickly look away, my hatred outweighing my empathy for him.

The teacher supervising our detention sits at his desk with the annoying sounds of his typing on the laptop keyboard reverberating throughout the room. I groan and put my head down, hoping that the next forty-five minutes will be over soon. When they finally are, I couldn't have gotten out of that room any faster.

"Alexa, wait!" At the sound of Matt's voice calling after me, I grip my bag tighter and start walking faster.

"Alexa!" he calls again.

"Leave me alone, Matt." I make a sharp right turn and enter the school's main hallway as the doors leading to the student parking lot coming into view. I angrily push through them and start speed walking to my car.

"Just hear me out!" he yells desperately, making me stop abruptly to turn around and face him.

"There's nothing you can ever say to me that will make up for what you did to Cam." He's about three feet away from me now. Being this close to him, I can see the prominent bags under his eyes. I can see how bloodshot his eyes are and how the red streaks through the white of his eyes remind me of lightning. Cam loved lightning; she loved the fact that lightning was so beautiful but can be so deadly when it struck. I shake my head and turn on my heel, heading towards my car.

"Please," he pleads as he runs after me and grabs my arm.

"Let go of me, Matt!" I try to rip my arm from his grasp, but he just tightens his grip.

"Not until you listen to my side of the story," he says.

"Let go of me," I repeat.

"Alexa, please . . ."

"Get your hands off of her!" We both turn our heads to see Blake, who's always there when I need him, with his lacrosse stick in hand and an angry look on his face. Matt lets go of me immediately and his eyes widen as he looks at the spot on my arm where his hand is now imprinted in bright red.

"I-I'm so sorry," he stutters.

"Leave before I do something I won't regret." Blake stands in front of me as if to shield me from anything and everything.

"I'm sorry," Matt says again before running off.

"Are you okay? Did he hurt you?" Blake questions, dropping his things to take my arm, which will no doubt be purple by tomorrow.

"I'm fine. It's just a bruise," I mumble.

"Just a bruise? He shouldn't have put his hands on you," he replies angrily.

"I don't think he even realized he was hurting me," I say, confused as to why I'm even trying to defend him.

"I don't want to see him near you again," he whispers.

"You and me both." I don't realize that we've somehow gotten closer to each other or that we're even moving until my back is pressed against my car. We stare at each other for a minute and the angry look in his eyes soften.

"How was detention?" He smirks.

"Let's just say I don't plan on ever getting detention again," I reply. "What are you still doing here anyway? School's out for the next two weeks."

"Coach held an intensive training session since we'll be out on break." A cold breeze passes by, making me shiver and causing loose strands of hair to blow out of my ponytail and across my face.

"You should head home," he says as he tucks the loose strands behind my ear. I can feel my face heat up. "I don't need you catching a cold."

"I'll see you soon. I'm sure your sisters will come up with some crazy adventure and drag us along."

"That's Alison and Madison for you." He laughs. I smile as I get into my car.

"Later, Harper."

"Later, Parker."

I watch as he picks up his lacrosse stick and bag from the floor before driving off.

What am I getting myself into?

* * *

I'm in my bed under piles of cozy blankets and getting ready to watch on Netflix for the rest of the night when the girls call me to pitch their latest idea.

"Let's go ice skating!" Alison screams through the phone. I have to hold it away from my ear.

"How about no," I reply.

Despite my years of cheer, when it comes to skating, I have the grace of a giant.

"It'll be fun!" Madison chimes in.

"Guys, last time I went ice skating, my butt was sore for about a week from the millions of times that I fell."

"It isn't really ice skating if you don't fall on your butt," Alison replies.

"Do I have to go? I kind of had plans tonight."

"Watching Netflix all night can wait. You have all winter break to do that. Besides, we've convinced Blake and a few other guys to go. We need some estrogen to balance out all the testosterone," Alison says.

"And we can go back to our house after for a sleepover with hot chocolate and s'mores," Madison adds.

"Fine." I sigh. "I'll go, but only because you're promising hot chocolate and s'mores."

"Great! We're already outside so hurry up." The line goes dead. I groan as I fling off the pile of blankets and make my way to my closet to put together an outfit.

Since ice rinks are always cold, I decide on jeans, a sweater, and a jacket to go over it. I pack a small bag since I'll be staying over at the girls' house tonight. I grab my phone and keys before heading into my parents' room where they're snuggled up and watching Netflix.

Oh, how I'd kill to be back in my bed right now.

"Hey, would it be okay if I stay over at the girls' house tonight?" I ask and they look up at me and smile.

"Of course," my mom says.

"Just check in every now and then so we know you're okay," my dad adds.

"I will. Love you, guys!" I reply quickly, and I hear them call out that they love me too as I rush downstairs, not wanting to keep the girls waiting for much longer.

"There's our little delinquent!" Madison grins as I get into their car.

"It was just detention." I roll my eyes.

"Ready to have fun tonight?" Madison asks too enthusiastically as she pulls out of my driveway.

"If you call falling and embarrassing myself in front of people fun, then sure. Who's all gonna be there besides Blake?" I inquire, the thought of seeing Blake tonight making my heart beat a little faster.

"Caleb, Braden, Evan, and Noah." Alison blushes when she says Noah's name, but I don't take the opportunity to make fun of her for it when I hear Evan's name.

"You guys invited Evan?"

"Yeah, why not?" they reply in unison.

"Maybe because he's interested in me and I am in no way interested in him!" I scream as if it's the most obvious thing in the world, which kind of is because I've told them that I'm not interested in him.

"That's because you haven't given him a chance," Madison says.

"And why exactly aren't you interested in him?" Alison questions.

Because I'm interested in your brother! I want to scream at them, but after the time they sat me down the night Blake stormed out of my house, I'm not sure it's such a good idea to tell them anything yet.

"Because trust me when I say that Evan isn't the guy for me," I say instead.

"Well, it's not like we can disinvite him, so you'll just have to put up with him for tonight."

I feel kind of bad for thinking about Evan as someone to be tolerated, but I'm just not interested in him in the way he is in me, and the sooner he realizes that, the better it will be for the both of us.

We arrive at Snow's Ice Rink where Caleb and Braden are already waiting. Caleb scoops Madison into his arms and spins her around. I try not to roll my eyes at how dramatic he is. Alison and Braden give each other a friendly hug. I smile at how they're still on good terms even though things didn't work out between them.

"Long time no see," someone says from behind me. I turn around to see Evan with Noah by his side.

"Hey." I smile. "I know. I've just been really busy lately."

"Well, I'm glad you could make it tonight." He gives me his blindingly white smile. Before he can say anything else, Madison makes an announcement.

"Blake got caught up in doing something for our mom, so he told us we can just get our skates and he'll meet us in the rink."

We all nod in response and head inside to get our skates. I'm still not sure about this whole ice skating thing, and it doesn't help that I'm even struggling to get them on.

"I can't believe you agreed to come ice skating," Braden says as he kneels down in front of me and helps me get my skates on. "You suck at ice skating."

"I actually had plans to stay home and watch Netflix all night, but you know how the girls are."

Once we manage to get both skates on, he extends his arm to help me stand up.

"Remember when we were little and our parents took us ice skating and you fell and lost your front tooth?" He laughs at the memory.

"I was lucky it wasn't my permanent tooth, and that's exactly why you're going to hold my hand and make sure I don't lose a tooth again."

I watch as everyone gets on to the ice with ease and pray that I don't slip and fall. Braden links his arm in mine and slowly guides me on to the ice.

"Braden, I'm not so sure about this," I say as my legs start to wobble.

"I won't let you fall, just move your feet left, then right, like this." He demonstrates how to do it. I slowly mimic his actions until I start to get the hang of it.

"Okay. I'm going to let go of you now, and you're going to follow me to the other side of the rink where everyone else is," he says.

"Braden, you better not," I warn but he lets go of me anyway. I stand still; I'm scared that if I make another move, I will fall on my face. "Braden!" I scream after him as he laughs and skates away.

"You are such a jerk!" I groan as I extend my arms out in front of me and try to reach for the wall or anything to hold on to. *Just wait till I get my hands on you, Braden.*

I slowly try to make my way to the wall, but once my legs start to wobble, I go still again.

Note to self: never let Alison and Madison convince you to go ice skating again.

"Here, let me help you." Evan gently grabs my arm and helps me to the wall. Once I grab on to it and am sure that I'm not going to fall, I let out a breath of relief.

"Thanks," I say graciously.

"No problem. I didn't think you would be bad at ice skating." He laughs.

"I'm like Bambi trying to walk for the first time," I joke.

"So I was wondering if you maybe wanted to go see a movie with me this weekend?"

Wow, straight to the point.

"Evan, you're a really nice guy," I start uneasily. "But I don't think that's a great idea." The hopeful look on his face immediately disappears and I feel bad knowing that it's because of me.

"You don't like me, do you?" he asks.

"No, it's not that. It's just—" I look around for anyone who can get me out of this mess, but everyone is on the other side of the rink. I look towards the entrance, and that's when my eyes land on Blake who must have just arrived.

"It's just I'm not the one you want to be here with," Evan mumbles as he follows my gaze.

"What—"

"I see the way you look at him," he cuts me off. "And I see the way he looks at you. I've seen it since the night of the lacrosse game and even at the diner." He stuns me with his revelation, and I search my mind for something—anything to say.

"Evan, I—"

"It's okay. I get it." He forces a smile.

"Evan, I'm so sorry if I led you on in any way." I find myself apologizing though I don't know why. I haven't done anything to make Evan think or believe that something is going to happen between us, but here I am, apologizing when I'm not at fault.

"Alexa, it's okay. I had a feeling that you weren't interested in me, but I guess there was just that small part of me that had hope."

"So no hard feelings?" I give him a hopeful smile.

"No hard feelings." We both look up as Noah calls out to him and he smiles at me before skating off.

As I watch him leave, it feels like a weight has been lifted off of my shoulders, then I realize that, once again, I'm stuck with no one to help me get to the entrance. I look to Blake who's still standing by the entrance and he laughs as Madison falls. It's as if he feels me watching him because he scans the rink until his eyes meet mine. He starts skating over to me with ease. I grow annoyed at how I'm literally the only person here who doesn't know how to skate. When he gets close enough, I start to move towards him. My legs start to wobble again, and before I can fall, he grabs on to me.

"Hey," I breathe out as I look up at him.

"Did they really leave you over here knowing you can't skate?" he questions.

"Yup, some friends they are." He shakes his head and smiles before swinging his arms around my waist.

"Let's get you off the ice before you hurt yourself."

He holds on to me tightly until we're off the ice and find ourselves sitting on a bench. I don't hesitate to take my skates off and wince as I notice how sore my feet are. I put my shoes back on before joining Blake at one of the tables in the concession area.

"I hope you don't mind me asking, but what's going on with you and Evan?" I'm a bit surprised by his question because Blake Harper isn't a straightforward guy, but I can't help but smile at the fact that he's curious about it.

"Nothing." I shrug. "He likes me, but I told him I'm not interested in him."

"And why is that?" He smirks, his green orbs stare right into mine from his spot across from me. I can imagine how pink my face must be tinted from his simple question, and for some reason, it makes me so nervous just thinking about the answer.

"I guess he saw that I was interested in someone else." Though he already knows, I don't tell him that he is *the* someone I'm interested in because saying it out loud will mean that I'm willing to hand over my heart completely, and I'm not sure I'm ready to do that yet.

We spend the next half an hour talking about anything and everything. It's crazy how naturally we fall in tune with each other even after all of my attempts to push him away—as if we've been friends all this time.

"Hey, guys, my butt is really sore from falling so I think it's time to head home." Madison walks up to us with a pained look on her face as she holds her skates in one hand while the other is intertwined with Caleb's. Blake and I are so busy talking that we don't notice everyone is already off the ice and hanging out near the arcade.

We all make our way to the exit and say our goodbyes. I still feel a bit bad for Evan, but he said there were no hard feelings and I have to remember that.

"Have you guys been hanging out at the tables the whole time?" Alison eyes the two of us. For some reason, a feeling of guilt and nervousness settles in the pit of my stomach.

"I helped Alexa off the ice since you guys left her and she couldn't skate," Blake replies for me.

"Well, let's get going!" she chirps. "We have s'mores and hot chocolate at home."

We make our way outside and I head towards the girls' cars when Blake stops me.

"You can ride with me if you want," he suggests.

"I would, but I'd rather not have your sisters interrogate us right now," I reply and he lets out a laugh.

"You're right." He nods. "I'll see you in a bit then."

"Bye." I smile, and he returns it before walking back to his car. I join the girls in the car, and they spend the short drive home talking about what a great night it's been.

Alison goes on and on about how Noah held her hand while they skated and Madison gushes over Caleb. I don't mind though, considering I would rather have them talk about themselves than them asking me questions I don't want to answer. When we arrive at their house, Blake is already sitting on their couch and changed into sweatpants and a shirt. His eyes shoot up towards us when we enter the living room. For what seems like the tenth time today, I feel my cheeks heat up when he looks at me.

After changing into something more comfortable, the girls and I take over the living room and decide to watch a movie. Blake went upstairs about twenty minutes ago, and I assume that he's probably asleep by now. The oven makes a beeping noise from the kitchen, signaling that our s'mores are done, and we all take in the aroma of the melted chocolate and marshmallow.

"Alexa, go upstairs and see if Blake wants any," Alison says as she puts on oven mittens.

"Are you sure he's not asleep by now?" I question.

"Blake is practically nocturnal. He's probably in his room reading a book or something," she replies. I nod before making my way up the stairs.

"His room is the second door on the left!" Madison yells after me.

The lights in the hallway are off and I can't see a thing. I bump into something and curse when I hear glass smash on to the floor. I immediately kneel down and start patting the floor, which probably isn't the smartest idea.

"Ow!" I hiss as I cut my hand on what feels like shards of glass.

"Alexa?" Blake calls out as the lights turn on.

His eyes travel to my bloodied hand, and he curses as he rushes over to me. It's a small cut in the palm in my hand yet so much blood.

"There's a first aid kit in the bathroom," he says after a moment of inspecting my hand. I follow him into the bathroom and he tells me to rinse my hand with water as he looks for the first aid kit.

"Found it. Can you sit up here for me?" He motions to a spot on the counter, and I hoist myself up, careful not to use my hand with the cut on it.

He grabs my hand and positions himself in front of me. I heat up at our close proximity. Blake doesn't seem to notice though because he's completely focused on my hand.

"This might sting a little." He takes an alcohol pad and slowly dabs it on to my cut. I wince a little at the pain, but it's nothing I couldn't handle. Nothing will ever compare to the pain I felt when I broke my ankle at a cheer competition.

"I could've done this myself, you know," I say as he finally puts a Band-Aid over it.

"A thank you would be nice." He smirks.

"Fine. Thank you." I laugh and watch as his eyes travel to the bruise that's formed on my arm from the incident with Matt yesterday.

"I hate seeing that bruise on you," he mutters. I look at the purple bruise surrounded by yellow.

"It'll go away soon," I say reassuringly. When I look back up at Blake, he's not looking at my arm anymore but at me.

"You have beautiful eyes," he whispers as he looks into them intently.

"I hate them," I say without thinking. "They're such a boring brown color."

"No they're not," he says indignantly. "You don't know how many times I've gotten lost in your eyes wondering about the girl behind them." Those words make a feeling I can't explain course throughout my body. Suddenly, it's as if we're magnets, pulling towards each other with the force of our longing.

"Blake . . ." I whisper as I find his arms wrapped around my waist and my arms around his neck. "What are we doing?"

"Something I've been wanting to do since that night." And just like magnets whose north and south poles can't help but attract towards each other, Blake's lips are on mine.

The kiss is soft and slow and grows into one of fiery passion. I'm the ember and Blake is the flame that ignites me. It's like nothing I've ever felt before, and when we pull away, we're out of breath as our foreheads rest against each other. We hear a noise and spring apart when we see Alison and Madison standing in the doorway with looks of shock and disbelief on their faces. *Oh, if the earth can just open up and swallow me whole right now.*

"You, guys . . ." Alison starts. "Have some explaining to do."

CHAPTER TWENTY-FOUR

The way the girls are staring at Blake and I as we sit across from them at the kitchen table is, to say the least, terrifying. I feel like I'm in an episode of CSI with the way they're staring us down. Right after they walked in on Blake and me in the bathroom, they immediately called an "emergency meeting" and practically dragged us downstairs. I look at Blake who's leaning back in his chair and is seemingly as cool as a cucumber while I, on the other hand, am freaking out.

"Blake, could you leave the room please," Madison says. When Blake doesn't make a move to leave, she narrows her eyes at him.

"Could you guys not be so dramatic?" he replies.

"Blake," Alison starts. "Leave. Now."

He huffs and exits the room, mumbling about how dramatic they are and how he's the only normal one in the family.

I watch as he leaves, screaming in my head at him to please not go, and when he's completely out of sight, I realize that I will have to be my own hero this time. When I turn back to Alison and Madison, they're completely focused on me.

"Can you guys please stop looking at me like I just committed some horrible crime?" I beg.

"How could you not tell us?" Alison says in a hushed voice. "Alexa, we thought you—"

"I know what I said," I huff, sinking into my chair. "But you guys don't understand."

"What do we not understand?" Madison asks. "Alexa, we caught you kissing our brother after we've watched you continuously push him away and hurt his feelings."

"It's not like that anymore!" I finally snap. They look at me, floored at my sudden outburst.

"Alexa, you don't know him like we do." The way those words come out of Alison's mouth make chills run up my spine.

"What did he do to make you guys think so lowly of him?" I question. I don't understand why they seem to be all for the idea of Blake and I that night in my bedroom on Thanksgiving, and now that I'm finally letting something happen with Blake, they're completely against it.

"He didn't do any—" Alison begins to speak but she cuts herself off. "It's not him, Alexa. It's you we're worried about." My heart drops to the bottom of my stomach and I feel like I've just been slapped.

"What?" I whisper.

"Alexa . . ." Madison's expression softens. "Blake's last relationship didn't end well, and we don't want to see our brother go through that again."

"I don't understand though." I run my hand through my hair. "What happened?"

"It's not our place to tell you," Alison says, letting me know that there is nothing they can do on their behalf. Blake's past is his story to tell and I have to respect that.

"I wouldn't hurt Blake, you guys know that, right?" My eyebrows draw together and the two look at each other as if considering whether or not to tell me what I need to hear.

"You just need to hear the whole story." They finally decide to leave me wondering and I sigh.

"How am I supposed to get him to open up to me about this?" I ask. I know that I've raised my volume a bit too much because Blake walks in and my heart goes haywire.

"About what?" he questions.

I turn to the green-eyed, dark-haired boy who's the entire reason for this conversation in the first place. His eyes are on me, expecting an answer, but all I can bring myself to do is turn to his sisters for help.

"Blake, if you and Alexa intend on getting serious, then you need to tell her about Talia," Alison says almost too quietly for any of us to hear, like she's afraid of Blake's reaction.

I instantly know why. when I see the look on Blake's face at the mention of that name.

"You guys told her?" he snaps, making all of us flinch. I've never seen him so angry, and this side of Blake is definitely something I've never seen before. His eyes soften as he sees the look on our faces but his gaze is still hard and his voice level.

"You guys had no right," he says as he glares at them.

"We just want to protect you!" they scream in unison.

"I'm your brother. I don't need my sisters to protect me. I'm supposed to be protecting you." He sighs and shakes his head before walking out of the kitchen.

We can hear the sound of the patio door sliding open, then slammed closed. I turn to the girls wide-eyed and even more confused.

"You should go check on him," Alison says quietly. "He probably doesn't want to talk to us right now."

I nod and take a deep breath before sliding out of the chair and make my way out of the kitchen and to the sliding glass doors of the patio. I can see Blake sitting in a hammock across their backyard with his back turned to me. He turns his head as he hears my footsteps on the grass and I offer him a smile.

"Mind if I join you?" I ask. He doesn't hesitate to scoot over, steadying the hammock as I sit down next to him.

The proximity between us makes a warmth spread throughout my body, and I try to ignore that feeling as I lean my head on his shoulders. We don't say anything for a few minutes.

We just sit there, staring up at the night sky.

"I guess I owe you an explanation," he finally says.

"You don't have to tell me if you don't want to," I reply.

No matter how much I want to know everything, I'm not going to pressure him to tell me if he's not ready.

"But I do want to tell you . . . I was going to tell you. I just thought it'd be on my own time."

"You know, your sisters think they're doing us a favor by doing whatever they're doing."

"They think they're protecting me." We sit in silence again as he lays his head on top of mine.

"Talia was my first real girlfriend back in Nebraska," he starts. I don't say anything, knowing that I'm finally going to hear everything.

"I was having a hard time with some kids here my freshman year, and my parents sent me to my uncle in Nebraska so I could take some time away from everything. As soon as I started school up there and joined the lacrosse team, all these girls started trying to get my attention, and Talia was the only one who wasn't." He stops and I nod for him to continue. I don't want to say anything yet, not until I hear the full story.

"Lacrosse season started, and she was always at every game, dragged along by her friends. Then, one day after a game we just bumped into each other and it took off from there. When everyone started to notice us hanging out, they started to pay attention to her and she was suddenly really popular. A couple of months later, I asked her to be my girlfriend and everything just went downhill from there.

"We were fine the first few months into our relationship. I adored her but then she started acting differently. She turned into someone I didn't recognize, but I stayed with her, which was stupid on my part. Junior year, she started getting all secretive, and one day after a lacrosse game, I found out why. She was hooking up with my closest friend at the time.

"I was hurt and broke up with her immediately. She didn't make the rest of my time there after our break up easy, so I got into the wrong crowd and became someone I didn't recognize. I hated that part of me, Alexa. I couldn't stand being there anymore so I finally came back here."

He moves so that he can look at me and I look at him, not knowing what to say. "So that's the story," he says as he stares at me intently, searching my face for any reaction. "I didn't want to tell you yet because I didn't want you to know about what I was like before I came back here."

The only thing going through my mind is how could anyone cheat on Blake? He's the definition of the perfect guy and anyone is lucky to have him.

"Funny what popularity can do to people," I mumble as I look down at my hands, wondering if that is the way I acted when I became cheer captain—if I ever made Cam feel like I changed.

"I want you to know that it's all in the past," he says, making me look up at him. "I'm over Talia and the entire situation." He takes a loose strand of hair hanging in front of my face and plays with it before tucking it behind my ear and cupping my cheek in his hand.

"From the day I saw you in that library, you had me entranced. I kept trying to tell myself that I should just leave you alone . . . that I couldn't let myself get hurt again. But it's you, Alexa. It's you I want." I take an intake of breath as we lean into each other and rest our foreheads together.

"Blake," I whisper. "I want this, whatever this is, but I can't lose another person in my life. So promise me, say you won't let go."

"I promise you I won't let go," he says, and for the second time that night, we're kissing, and it feels even more magical than the first.

He cups my face and I wrap my arms around his neck, pulling him closer. It's the kind of kiss that says everything that needs to be said. The kind of kiss that makes me feel happy and safe and tells me that everything will be okay, then the unexpected happens. We both somehow flip off of the hammock and land on the grass with Blake landing on top of me and holding himself up in a way that ensures he's not squishing me. We both stare at each other wide-eyed before we start to laugh and he comes down for another kiss.

Blake looks toward the patio doors and I follow his line of vision to see Alison and Madison watching us with smiles on their faces.

"We should probably go back inside," I say.

"Yeah, before they come out here and drag us inside." He laughs as he gets up and helps me up as well. We head towards the sliding glass doors and Alison immediately opens them.

"We're sorry for saying you guys weren't good for each other," Alison starts with a look of awe in her eyes.

"You guys couldn't be more perfect for each other," Madison adds. I smile at them as Blake and I step inside. "We realize now that Alexa would never hurt you like Talia did."

"No more deciding what's good for me," Blake states and they nod.

"We promise," they reply.

The rest of the night is spent eating s'mores, watching movies, and Blake and I stealing glances at each other. I don't know how to even begin to understand what is happening between us, but all I know is that I never want it to end.

CHAPTER TWENTY-FIVE

There are a few things I've learned about Blake these past few days.

First, he's selfless, always more concerned about the well-being of everyone else than his own and I love that about him.

Second, he makes the best waffles ever.

And third, he's really competitive.

"Damn it," he says as I beat him in 8 ball for what has to be the fifth time.

I'm at the Harper residence because the girls wanted to have another sleepover. Blake and I have been playing iMessage games for the last hour, and despite the fact that he's beat me in every other game, 8 ball happens to be the game he can't beat me in.

"I was so close." He groans.

"You were." I giggle.

"No one has ever beaten me in 8 ball."

"I guess you, Blake Harper, have met your match."

"Then I guess I have no choice but to surrender." He smirks at me and tosses his phone aside before leaning in for a kiss.

Now that we don't have to constantly worry about his sisters, kissing is something we seem to be doing a lot lately. We kiss any chance we get. If his kisses were a drug, I would be an addict. Each time we kiss, it feels like the first time all over again, and though whatever is going on between Blake and I has yet to be defined, I'm happy where we are. I've never had a real relationship before, and it's definitely something I don't want to rush into.

"Let's go to a party tonight!" Alison shouts as she walks in with Madison following closely behind her.

"No," Blake and I reply simultaneously.

We have surprisingly gone an entire week without the girls coming up with any one of their crazy outings, and I want it to stay that way.

"Come on! It's New Year's Eve. Do you really want to spend it staying in all night?" Madison says.

"Do you really want to spend it cramped between sweaty bodies of people who you don't even know and smell like weed and alcohol?" Blake counters.

"Okay, you have a point but still! We need to let loose before we have to go back to school again," Alison whines.

"I don't know . . ." I say.

Going to this party means we're bound to see some kids from school, and I'm definitely not up for that. Plus, no one really knows about Blake and me. It's not that I'm trying to keep it a secret; it's just I don't want our undefined relationship being exploited to the whole school and attracting any unnecessary attention or gossip.

"We're still going to go whether you guys come or not, it'd just be nice if you did," Madison says. Blake and I look at each other knowing that if we don't go to watch over them, they're bound to get themselves into some sort of trouble.

"Fine, we'll go," Blake starts. "But no drinking at all unless it's soda or water."

"Deal!" they squeal.

"Alexa, you can wear something from our closet," Alison says.

"What's wrong with what I have on?" I ask while looking down at my plain grey shirt and high-waisted jeans.

"Don't you want to wear something dressier?"

"I'll pass," I say. "I refuse to wear anything less than this in the cold weather."

"Well, at least help us choose something to wear," she says. I sigh as I get up from my spot on the couch and follow them upstairs and into their room.

"Black tube top or red tube top?" she questions as she holds up the two.

"The black one, but are you sure you want to wear that in this fifty-degree weather?" I question as I watch Alison throw on the black tube top.

"What do you think jackets are for?" She laughs as she slides her arms through a denim jacket before throwing her hair up into a ponytail.

Madison, the more practical one out of the two, opts for a cute V-neck sweater, which shows more cleavage than I could ever hope to have. On any other girl, it would have looked like too much but Madison makes it look classy as she slides on a coat over it.

"Time to get our party on!" she says excitedly.

"Yay," I reply as I follow them downstairs, making it obvious that I don't share in their excitement.

When we get downstairs, Blake is sitting on the couch, flipping through the channels on the television. He switches it off once he sees us. He must have changed while I was upstairs with the girls because he's traded in his sweats and shirt for a pair of black jeans and a sweatshirt, which, may I add, looks very good on him.

"Ready to go?" he asks and we all nod.

Before we head out the door, I grab my bomber jacket, which does nothing against the cold outside. We all hurry into Blake's car and he immediately blasts on the heat.

"So where is this party?" He turns to the girls who are sitting in the back seat and Alison's face turns slightly pink.

"It's at Noah's house actually," she replies.

Of course. We should have known. I resist the urge to tease her about it as Blake pulls out of their driveway and starts the route to Noah's house. Madison leans over to turn the radio on and flips through the stations before settling on an indie station.

She sings along quietly and I have to admit that she's a damn good singer. Good looks and talent, what can't this family do?

"Remember what I said," Blake says. "No drinking—"

"Unless it's soda or water," they interrupt him. "Yes, we know."

"And don't leave your drinks unattended. I've watched way too many of your high school drama shows to know what that leads to."

We arrive at the large house whose driveway is already packed with a variety of cars. We park across from the house a little down the street considering most of the space around the house is already taken.

"Okay, Dad. We get it." Alison rolls her eyes and we get out of the car.

They may find Blake's overprotectiveness annoying but I find it pretty cute. He's their brother and he's just doing what he said he's going to do which is to protect them. The girls walk ahead of us, and I laugh at how Alison rushes Madison with her, already wanting to see Noah.

She may deny that she is totally crushing on him, but her actions say otherwise. The party is just like I expected it to be but even more intense. There are people everywhere with red solo cups in hand while they wildly shake to the music. Yes, shake. It's not dancing; it's more like shaking. I can't remember the last time I came to a party. What I do know is that parties are, for a time, something I really enjoyed up until the moment I couldn't enjoy them.

I look around, noticing that the girls are already off to do their own thing. I turn to Blake who is still behind me, greeting some guys from the lacrosse team. I recognize most of them from the game, but there are some I don't remember seeing. Especially this tall dark-haired boy. His eyes are a gorgeous sparkling hazel color, but I'm sure that in the daylight, they're brighter and just as lovely. His skin is an almost golden caramel color but even with his extremely good looks, he has nothing on Blake.

I don't notice him staring at me until my eyes meet his, and I offer a friendly smile. He returns the gesture with a smirk.

"I'm going to go get a drink," Blake calls, breaking me out of whatever trance I'm in. "Do you want to come with me?"

"Sure." Blake holds my hand as we weave through the crowd.

Everyone is too cramped and too inebriated to notice us, and the dim lights definitely help. We push our way into the kitchen, which is still pretty crowded but better than the rest of the house. He grabs a water bottle from the fridge since alcohol is the only thing out on the counter. I hope that the girls didn't get here before us to sneak a drink. Cam and I were never drinkers, and I'm proud that we didn't let high school pressure us into doing what everyone else is doing. Why wake up with a killer headache and no recollection of what happened the night before when you can wake up perfectly fine and not worry about what happened that night?

"I hate coming to these things," Blake says.

"Too bad your sisters love dragging us to them," I joke.

"Speaking of my sisters, have you seen them at all since we got here?" The look on my face says it all and we both agree to split up to look for them.

It doesn't feel like we were here for that long. In fact, it feels like we have just gotten here, but as I check the time, I realize that we have already been here for almost an hour. Apparently, time works differently when you're at a party.

I find myself being pushed and tossed through the crowd like a tiny fish being tossed by the waves in the sea. I even have to elbow a few people to get through. I can't find the girls anywhere in the crowd so I turn to my right and head towards the stairs.

"I'm so sorry," someone says as a cold sticky liquid splashes on to my shirt.

One of the many reasons I hate parties.

I grit my teeth and take a moment to keep my cool before looking up. It's the dark-haired boy from earlier, and when he recognizes me, his eyes light up. Even the way his eyes sparkle can't mitigate how annoyed I am right now that my shirt is sticking to my skin.

"Hey, beautiful," he says, completely ignoring the fact that his drink is on my shirt.

"Listen, I am so not in the mood right now," I say as I motion to my shirt.

"Sorry about that. Why don't you follow me upstairs and I can . . . help you out." I narrow my eyes at him and I can feel myself starting to get even more annoyed.

Is this guy serious right now?

"I'm fine. I think I'm capable of helping myself." I start to move past him but he grabs my arm.

"Come on, don't be so difficult. I saw the way you were looking at me earlier."

"You were the one doing most of the looking." I yank my arm from his grasp.

"Playing hard to get, huh?" He smirks as he takes a step closer to me. "Let's just stop with the games and have some real fun." He circles his arm around my waist and tries to pull me forward. *Why do I always have the worst luck when it comes to situations like this one?*

"Dude, seriously. What don't you understand?" I scream.

"Julian, what the hell are you doing?" And just like that, always there when I need him is Blake. He gently pulls me into him and stares Julian down.

"She your girlfriend or something?" Julian asks as he stares between Blake and me and acts like he wasn't just about to force me upstairs with him.

"Yeah, she is," he says. I'm too busy watching him clench his fists to even notice that he called me his girlfriend.

"Wow, Blake!" Julian laughs. "So you really do like the crazy ones, huh?" I furrow my brows and wonder what he means by that while Blake takes a step forward.

"I'd watch my mouth if I were you," he says.

"Or what?" Julian taunts as he, too, takes a step forward.

Alison and Madison suddenly appear out of nowhere. I think about the fact that we only came to this party to make sure they don't get into trouble, yet here's Blake and I who are in our own trouble. I give them a where-were-you-guys look while they respond with a what-is-going-on look.

"I already kicked your ass once, I can do it again," Blake says and, knowing where this is going, I grab his arm.

"Blake, don't," I say. "He's not worth it."

People are starting to focus on us now, and I'm definitely not going to give them a show.

"Blake," I plead. "Let's just go."

"You should listen to your girlfriend, Harper, before I do something I won't regret." Julian smiles as he says it. There's something about the sinister look in his eyes that gives me bad vibes and sends a chill up my spine.

Blake must feel it, too, because he glares at Julian before turning away.

"Let's go," he says to us. The girls and I hurriedly make our way to the exit of the house.

Everyone must have realized that they aren't going to get a New Year's show because they just resume what they are doing before as if nothing ever happened.

"Where were you, guys?" I ask the girls once we get into the car.

"We were with Noah," Alison starts. "What was all of that about?"

I don't really have an explanation for what just happened between Blake and Julian so I turn to him.

"Julian was just being a tool as usual," he replies as he starts driving back to their house.

I know that there's something he's not saying. I want to press him to tell us, but he gives me a look that says he'll explain later.

When we get back to their house, I follow the girls upstairs to their room and ask to take a shower to wash off the sticky residue of the drink that was spilled on me. Once I'm clean and changed into something more comfortable, I join them on Alison's bed for some girl talk.

"I think I like Noah," Alison says. "Like really like him."

"Really? I couldn't tell," Madison replies sarcastically and Alison rolls her eyes.

"You did make it pretty obvious," I add.

"Geez, I hope I didn't look desperate." She facepalms and groans as she rests her head on a pillow.

"I mean, Noah also made it pretty obvious that he likes you, too, so I don't think you have anything to worry about," Madison reassures her.

"He asked me out tonight," she admits but she doesn't sound as excited about that as she should be.

"What did you say?" I ask her.

"I didn't say anything! When he asked me, I got so nervous and then we saw the commotion with Julian and Blake, and we just sort of rushed towards you. He probably thinks I don't want to go out with him."

"Just text him and clear everything up," Madison says.

"Yeah, I think I will."

We sit in comfortable silence for a while before I finally say what's been on my mind since we left the party.

"I think Blake called me his girlfriend tonight." Alison and Madison immediately jolt up.

"He asked you to be his girlfriend?" they ask simultaneously.

"No, but when the whole incident was taking place, Julian asked if I was Blake's girlfriend and Blake said that I was. I'm sure he only said it as a spur-of-the-moment kind of thing."

"Are you kidding!" Alison starts. "Alexa, Blake is head over heels for you. Why wouldn't he want you to be his girlfriend?"

"Did you talk to him about it?" Madison asks.

"Not yet," I reply, chagrined.

"What are you waiting for? Go talk to him!" she exclaims.

I immediately get up and walk down the hallway to Blake's room.

His door is cracked open and his lights are on so I assume he's still awake. When I open the door, he's on his bed reading a book with glasses sitting on the bridge of his nose.

"You wear glasses?" I ask, surprised.

"Only when I read." He smiles up at me as he takes his glasses off and closes his book, which I notice is a copy of *War and Peace*.

"I think they're cute," I reply as I crawl on to his bed and sit in front of him.

"Yeah? Maybe I should wear them more often." He leans in and pecks me on my lips. I fight the urge to wrap my arms around him to pull him back in.

Talk first, kiss later.

"I want to talk to you about what happened at the party," I say.

"I figured."

"It just . . . it seemed like you and Julian already had some unresolved issues?" It comes out more like a question and Blake sighs.

"Remember that day I came to the hospital to see you, and my fist was bruised because I punched a guy who was talking bad about you in the locker room?" he asks and I nod. "Julian was that guy and seeing him grab you like that just made me so mad," he says angrily and I grab on to his hand.

"Hey, it's okay. I don't care about Julian or anything he's said about me."

"Good because nothing he says is true." He pulls me into him and I lay my head on his chest as he wraps his arms around me.

But then, I remember that there's one more thing I need to ask him about. I prop myself up on his chest so that I'm looking at him.

"So girlfriend, huh?" I ask. His eyes widen as his face turns slightly red.

Is Blake Harper blushing? And because of me?

"I'm sorry if that made you alarmed. I mean, I know we never made anything official but if you're not ready to be my girlfriend, I understand and I'm so—" I cut him off by pressing my lips to his, smiling at how flustered he is.

"Blake," I say when we pull away. "I'd be happy to be your girlfriend."

"Yeah?" he asks, still kind of flustered.

"Yeah." I laugh. This time, he's the one who pulls me in for a kiss.

I can hear fireworks go off somewhere outside, which is ironic because that's how it feels kissing Blake—like fireworks and every good thing in this world. Then, as they always do, Alison and Madison burst into the room, interrupting our kiss.

"Happy New Year!" they scream as they jump on to Blake's bed.

"Happy to see that you guys will still be interrupting us in the new year," Blake mumbles. I laugh as Alison throws a pillow at him.

"Happy New Year," I whisper.
"Happy New Year," he whispers back.

CHAPTER TWENTY-SIX

Winter break is coming to an end, and it's unfortunately time to return to school. Quite frankly, I don't know what to expect. I'm sure that people have heard about Blake claiming me as his girlfriend at the party, and I know that once everyone actually sees us together, news of our relationship will spread like wildfire.

It isn't that I don't want people to know about Blake and me; it's that I don't want to ruin his reputation. What will people say when they hear he's dating the once most popular girl in school turned mental case? He must sense that something is wrong because he grabs my hand with his free one and laces his fingers through mine. Blake offered to take me to school today and I agreed. The girls sit in the back doing who knows what on their phones. My bet is that they're texting Noah and Caleb.

"What's wrong?" he asks.

"Are you sure you want people to know we're dating?" I blurt out, causing the girls to look up from their phones and a look of confusion to take place on Blake's features.

"Do you not want to be my girlfriend?" he asks hesitantly. The girls have yet to say something. It's as if they both decided that, for once, this is none of their business.

"No!" I scream, beginning to get flustered. "I didn't mean it like that. I love being your girlfriend, but what if I ruin your reputation when everyone finds out you're dating the school's mental case?"

"Alexa," Blake says sternly as he parks and takes my face into his hands. "You are not a mental case, and I can care less what people think. You're my girlfriend and I want the whole world to know. I'll scream it at the top of my lungs if I have to."

"I just don't want the guys on the team to give you trouble for dating me," I whisper.

"I don't care what they think. They can give me trouble all they want, but as long as I have you, I'm happy." I smile at that and, for a moment, it's just Blake and I, but then, the girls cough and I remember that we're not alone.

"I ship you guys so hard," Alison says, ruining the moment.

"Who knew Blake could be so romantic?" Madison adds while Blake and I roll our eyes.

"The bell is going to ring soon. We should head in," Blake says, giving me a reassuring look.

We all get out of the car, and I tug my jacket sleeves down some more as the cold air hits. The lawn isn't littered with teens like it usually is, so they all must have gone inside to escape the cold. That, or something must be happening. When we walk in, I expect eyes to be on us but their attention is fixed on something else. I look down the hall and what I see definitely takes me by surprise. Alison and Madison drop their jaws as they watch Paige make out with Evan in front of the entire school.

"Is that allowed?" Madison starts. "That shouldn't be allowed."

As I watch the show they're putting on, the only thing I can feel is disappointment. Not at the fact that Evan has clearly moved on from me because, trust me, I have zero feelings for the guy. I'm disappointed at the fact that a nice guy like Evan would settle for someone like Paige.

"Talk about opposites attract," Alison mutters as if reading my thoughts.

"Tell me about it," Madison and I reply simultaneously.

"Well, at least everyone's attention isn't on us," I offer.

"Speaking of, let's get you to class while everyone is still distracted," Blake says. I nod as our hands intertwine while we make our way to the other hallway where the girls and I's first-hour class is.

"I'll see you guys at lunch." He kisses me on my forehead as the bell rings. I smile as I watch him walk away. We walk into our physics class; we're the first to take our seats.

"We get our midterm grades today," Alison says nervously.

"I'm sure you guys did great," I say encouragingly.

The rest of the class piles in. When everyone is quiet, Mr. Bronson gets straight to the point.

"I know all of you are anxious to see your results so let's get straight to it." He grabs a stack of papers and starts handing them down each row.

"Yes! I got an eighty!" Alison whisper-yells.

"Eighty-eight!" Madison says excitedly, and I can only hope my grade is just as good.

"Ninety-two!" I say when I get my paper, my heart jumping in my chest. I was sure I was going to fail, but it seems like all of my studying has really paid off.

We spend the rest of the class hour going over the answers and so on for every other class. I'm extremely proud of myself for passing all of my midterms, and I find myself excited to tell Blake all about it. He's already sitting at the table when we get there and I slide into the seat next to him.

"How was class?" he asks with his signature smile that I can't get enough of.

"It was great! I passed all of my midterms!" I reply excitedly.

I know I'm probably way too enthusiastic about this, but after what's happened the last few months, I don't think it's possible for me to get back on track with everything, let alone pass all of my midterms with a grade of ninety percent or higher.

"I knew you would," he says. I lean in to give him a quick peck on the lips, not wanting to draw any attention the way Paige and Evan did this morning with their show. It still baffles me how Evan can ever be with Paige.

"Noah!" Alison calls out as he walks into the cafeteria. She waves her arms, motioning for him to come over. He smiles at her as he slides into the seat next to her. He then proceeds to call Evan over, and I groan as I see Paige tag along.

"I was having such a great day, and now, I have to deal with Paige," I groan.

"Just pretend she's not here," Blake whispers, which is easier said than done.

Paige is like that pesky annoying fly that somehow zooms into your house as soon as you open the door and takes forever to get rid of.

"Hey," Evan greets to no one in particular, deliberately not meeting my gaze.

No one really acknowledges Paige, and we all sort of sit in an awkward silence as she stares me down. I resist the urge to challenge her scrutiny. *No fights today, Alexa.*

"So, you and Paige, huh?" Madison says, breaking the ice.

"Don't we just make the cutest couple?" Paige says, feigning sweetness. I snort. She fixes her gaze on me once again and narrows her eyes.

"Something funny, Alexa?" she asks. The way she says my name is enough to make my blood boil.

"I'm just surprised is all," I reply.

"Why is it such a surprise that someone like me is dating someone like Evan?" Everyone around the table is quiet, even Evan, and the growing tension is so thick you could cut it with a knife.

"That's exactly the point. Evan is Evan and you . . . well, you're you." I shrug.

Blake grabs my hand under the table and squeezes it as if to tell me not to entertain her, but once Paige gets going, there's no stopping her.

"At least I could get Evan to talk to me of my own doing and not because of some bet," she spits out and I furrow my brows.

"Paige," Evan whispers to her sternly but she ignores him.

"What is that supposed to mean?" I ask, looking between the two of them.

"Paige, don't—" Evan starts but Paige cuts him off.

"Oh, you didn't know? The only reason Evan started talking to you in the first place was because the guys bet him that he couldn't get you to sleep with him?" Paige says smugly.

"Is this true?" I demand, staring straight at Evan.

My stomach drops when he doesn't say anything. I can feel my face heating up in anger but, before I can say anything else, Blake abruptly stands up.

"Let's go," he says to the girls and me, seemingly just as angry as I am. He clenches his fists but I can tell he's trying to control himself because I know he doesn't want to have to fight Evan.

Seeing Blake so self-restrained does nothing to calm my urge to pounce across the table and slap both Evan and Paige across the face. I guess they are perfect for each other after all. They deserved each other.

"Let's go, Alexa," Madison says as she and Alison listen to Blake. "As much as I want to punch her in her face, too, we can't afford a fight right now."

I nod slowly and grab my things. I can feel the pressure building up behind my eyes. The girls both place their hands on the small of my back as they guide me out of the cafeteria.

"You're lucky I don't kick your ass right now." I hear Blake say, but I can't even focus on the sound of his voice because all I can think about is how Evan only talked to me because of a bet.

154

How the boys at this school think I'm something to bet on and how they make a mockery of me and what I've been through.

The girls pull me into a quiet hallway and look at me with concern-filled eyes. Blake follows after us and he immediately embraces me. The feeling of his arms around me is enough to help me blink the tears away.

"How could he do something like that?" Alison questions angrily.

"I knew that Paige was up to something when she came over," Madison says.

"Can we just go?" I ask, not at all wanting to be at this school any longer.

Every time I come to this place, there will be always something wrong and I end up in some type of predicament. I should've just switched schools when I had the chance, but it's almost the end of the year and college applications are due so it's already way too late in the year to switch. I ask Blake to take me home, and the car ride to my house is spent in silence. Blake grips the steering wheel tightly with one hand, and he clenches his other one as if contemplating whether or not to turn back around and actually deliver on his threat to Evan.

I take his hand in mine and he relaxes, allowing me to entwine my fingers with his. He looks at me, and the hard look in his eyes softens. It still gets to me how I have that effect on him. When we get to my house, the girls stay in the car as they give Blake and I some privacy while he walks me to my door.

"Alexa," he starts and I shake my head.

"It's okay. You didn't know about the bet. They obviously excluded you from it because they knew you would stop it from happening," I say.

"I just hate the way they talk about you. I can't stand it and I hate how nothing I do can stop them from doing it."

"Blake, it's not your fault," I say to him as I circle my arms around his waist and look up at him. "It's just the way high school is."

"Then why do I feel like it is? They only talk about you because they know that it gets to me. What if it's me that's ruining your reputation?"

"My reputation is already ruined. It was ruined way before I met you, but I'll be fine. We'll be fine."

"Alexa, I—" he starts but then abruptly stops himself.

"What is it?" I ask him.

He shakes his head, and instead of saying anything else, he pulls me in for one of those mind-shattering kisses. I know what he wanted to say but didn't, but that's okay because this kiss says everything.

Blake is mine, I'm his, and that's enough.

CHAPTER TWENTY-SEVEN

It's been weeks since school started again, and I can't wait for the day that I get to leave this place for good. I haven't seen Evan since the day I found out what kind of person he really is. My guess is that he's avoiding me just as much as I'm avoiding him, which is probably for the best as I'm not sure I can talk to him without punching him in his stupid face.

Paige, on the other hand, has no problem showing her face. Every time I pass her in the hallway, she has this satisfied smirk on her face. It takes everything in me not to slap it off. After all, it's almost the end of the year and it's time to start thinking about college. I don't need a fight to be on my record nor do I want detention again.

And then there's Matt. We haven't interacted since that day in the parking lot. Every time we make eye contact, he gives me this pleading look but he's never actually come up to me to talk, which is probably because Blake acts like my bodyguard—always with me wherever I go besides my classes.

"Guess who has a date for Valentine's Day!" Alison squeals as she sits next to me under the shade of our school's sycamore tree. It's our new lunch spot and is way more peaceful than the noisy cafeteria.

"Let me guess," I say, feigning thought. "You?"

"Noah's taking me out to dinner!"

"Must be nice," Madison starts. "Caleb has yet to ask me out for Valentine's Day."

"I'm sure he will," I say, not trying to give away that I know something she doesn't.

"He better. Valentine's Day is tomorrow."

"What about you?" Have any plans with our brother?" Alison says as she takes a sip of her water and wiggles her perfectly shaped eyebrows.

"Well, Blake wanted to take me out for dinner, but I told him I'd much rather stay in and spend the night watching movies with him," I reply before taking a bite out of my wrap.

"You guys are so boring." Alison laughs and I throw a carrot at her.

"Sorry I'm late," Blake says as he joins us. "A teacher dropped all of her papers on the floor so I stayed back to help her pick them up." *Why was he so perfect?*

"What did I miss?" He looks between the three of us, and we weirdly refuse to let him in on our Valentine's Day conversation so I start the topic of college applications.

"I already sent mine out," Alison informs us. I envy her for a second at how on track she is.

"What about you?" I turn to Blake who visibly tenses at the question and my eyebrows draw together. "What school are you applying to?"

Blake's face grows a shade paler at my question and the way his eyes flicker to his sisters, I know that there is something he's not telling me. I can tell it's not something bad though, considering the grins on the girls' faces as they raise their eyebrows at Blake.

"Stanford," he mumbles. I almost choke on my water.

"That's amazing!" I hug him and he lets out one of his glorious laughs.

"I haven't gotten in yet, babe." He chuckles and I can't help but heat up at the nickname. He's never called me anything other than my name before, and I wasn't a fan of pet names . . . until now.

"Babe?" I take advantage of the opportunity to tease him and his cheeks begin to flush.

"Oh, uh . . . sorry, I didn't—" I cut off his apologies with a quick kiss to the lips and he instantly relaxes.

"Don't apologize." I smile. "I like it."

"I envy you, guys." Madison gazes at us. "I wish Caleb would grow a pair and ask me out already."

As if on cue, I see my idiot cousin creeping up behind Mads with a bouquet of pink roses in hand. My cousins can be a pain but they can also be really sweet when they want to be.

"Madison." I nod behind her and the smile that appears on her face as she turns to see Caleb makes my heart warm.

"What are you doing here?" She squeals in excitement, though it's obvious that this is what she's been waiting for.

"Well, Valentine's day is tomorrow and I was wondering if you wanted to go on a picnic with me?"

"I'd love to!" She hugs him, accepting the roses.

"Great! Well, I've got to go before Mr. Maxwell notices that I'm gone, but I'll call you." He stands from his spot on the ground.

"Caleb, did you really sneak out of class to drive over here and ask Madison out?" I ask.

"Yes, I did." He nods proudly before giving Madison a kiss and taking off.

"You happy now?" Blake asks her. She nods excitedly, hugging the bouquet of flowers as we all laugh.

* * *

The rest of the day is filled with Valentine's Day surprises, and I can't wait to get home and spend the rest of my day watching Netflix while wrapped up in a fuzzy blanket. Just as I'm about to start my binge-watching, the doorbell rings and I wiggle myself out of my blanket burrito before shuffling downstairs to answer the door. I swing the door open, surprised to see a pizza delivery guy with a smile on his face as he holds the red delivery bag in his hand.

"Hi," he greets. "Did you order a large pepperoni with extra cheese and stuffed crust?"

"No." I furrowed my eyebrows at the guy, evidently confused. "I didn't order a pizza."

"Oh," he says. "Some guy called and ordered this. He paid for it and set this as the address for the delivery." *Large pepperoni with extra cheese and stuffed crust. Whoever did this knew my regular order.*

"Did you by any chance get the guy's name?" I ask, trying to figure out who would send this, and my thoughts only seem to wrap around one possible culprit.

"No, but he did give special directions to write something on the inside of the box." He slides the pizza out of the carrier and hands it to me. "It's already paid for, so my advice to you is to just enjoy it."

I take the pizza from him with no hesitation, and he smiles before heading back to his car. It takes me a minute to take in all that's happened. When the delicious smell of pepperoni begins to penetrate my senses, I shut the door and head into the kitchen. I don't hesitate to open the box and that's when I see the message written on the inside.

Be My Valentine?

I didn't notice that the actual pizza itself was decorated with a pepperoni heart in the center, and my heart almost jumps out of my chest at the gesture. This is the most romantic thing I've ever gotten. I'm about to reach for a slice when my phone vibrates in my back pocket. I unlock it, sliding to answer the call.

"Did you get my gift?" Blake's voice sounds through the phone, confirming my suspicions.

"Yes." I smile. "How'd you know it was my favorite?"

"Well, the other night when you ordered pizza, I may or may not have made a point to remember the order and I may or may not have done that at every food place we've been to together just to know what you like."

"Blake Harper, you are the sweetest." Knowing he pays that much attention to every little thing makes my heart flutter.

"Only for you, Alexa Parker." He chuckles through the phone and I gush at the sound.

"So have you thought of an answer to my question?" I look back at the box, seeing the message.

"Blake, I'm pretty sure being your girlfriend means I'm automatically your valentine."

"I know, but it made the whole 'sending you a pizza thing' a lot cuter, you have to admit."

"Well, my answer is yes." I laugh. "I'll be your Valentine."

"Perfect. I can't wait to spend all of tomorrow with you," he says, causing a plethora of butterflies to erupt in my stomach.

"Me too," I reply. I turn my head towards the door as I hear keys jingle.

"My parents are home. I'll talk to you later," I say in a hushed whisper before hanging up.

"How's my favorite daughter?" my dad chirps as he walks into the kitchen and pecks me on the cheek before setting down his briefcase.

"Dad, I'm your only daughter."

"Exactly," he says.

I shake my head with a smile before turning my attention towards my mom when she walks in.

"Hey, sweetie," she greets as she throws her keys on to the countertop.

It's then I realize that for the first time in a while, both of my parents are home early and at the same time. I have been so used to them working late that it's a shock seeing them both here at this time.

"How was school?" she asks.

"School was school." I sigh. "What are you guys doing home so early?"

"Your mother and I took the rest of today and tomorrow off so I can treat her to Valentine's Day dinner," my dad replies as he circles his arms around her waist. "You can come if you want. I could take both of my favorite girls out to dinner."

"Oh, I can't. I have plans," I say awkwardly and curse myself for giving myself away.

My parents don't exactly know about Blake and I yet, and though I know they won't have a problem with it, I just never have the chance to tell them and I definitely wasn't expecting to tell them like this.

"With who?" My mother raises an eyebrow at me and I avoid my dad's suspicious gaze.

"Just a friend." I turn around and pick up a slice of my pizza, mostly to hide how red my face must be.

"The same friend who sent you that pizza?" my dad asks as he eyes the words written on the inside of the box and I quickly shut it.

"It's Blake Harper, isn't it?" my mother questions. My silence and the way my face heats up even more is her answer.

"I knew it!" she screams. "You owe me a massage," she says to my dad with a satisfied look on her face.

"You guys bet on me and Blake?!" I exclaim in disbelief.

"Your father believed you when you told us the night of your dance that you didn't like Blake, but I didn't. Mother's instinct." She points to her head and winks at me.

"Unbelievable," I mutter.

"What's unbelievable is that my baby girl has a boyfriend and didn't even tell me," he replies.

"I'll be eighteen next month."

"You are still a baby."

"It's not even that big of a deal!"

"I want to talk to this Blake Harper."

"So you can embarrass me?"

"Oh come on, I'm not going to embarrass you! It's a rite of passage for a girl's dad to scare the shit out of their boyfriend."

"That is so not happening."

My mother watches us go back and forth with amusement in her eyes before she decides that she's seen enough.

"Okay, stop it," she starts. "Alexa, we have no problem with you dating, but we do need to be able to talk to him and it would have been nice if you told us."

"I know. I meant to but it was never a good time," I say apologetically.

They look at each other and seem to be having a telepathic conversation before my dad seems to give in to whatever my mom is telling him.

"You can spend your Valentine's Day with him tomorrow," my dad says. It's almost like the thought of me going out with a boy physically pains him.

"But you should expect the Harpers to be over for dinner this weekend," my mom starts.

"The last time we saw them was Thanksgiving and I think the news of you and Blake dating calls for a reunion."

I groan but nod and practically sigh in relief when they finally decide to stop interrogating me and head upstairs. I grab the box of pizza and smile when I open it to re-read the message written inside.

* * *

School goes by surprisingly fast the next day. I wait till my parents leave for their "romantic dinner" before calling Blake over. I know that they are trying to be inconspicuous about their lingering behind to try and catch him as he arrived, but I made sure to shoo them out because the last thing I need is my dad playing the hurt-my-daughter-and-I'll-kill-you act.

Using whatever time I have left before Blake arrives, I make sure that there are enough pillows and fuzzy blankets to choose from as that is a necessity when watching movies. The doorbell rings and I do a once-over in one of the decorative mirrors hung on the wall before rushing to the door and swinging it open. Blake is holding a large paper bag, which seems to be filled to the top with a copious amount of snacks, looking as handsome as ever. He grins as I usher him in. He sets the bag on the kitchen island before wrapping his arms around my waist and pulling me into him.

"Happy Valentine's Day," he whispers. Our faces are so close together that our noses are touching and his lips are barely an inch away.

"Happy Valentine's Day," I whisper back before pressing my lips against his. It's a slow yet passionate kiss. I almost whimper when he pulls away. If he noticed, he doesn't show it because he begins to unpack all of the snacks.

"I got all of your favorites and also some other stuff that I thought would be cool to try." I watch him carefully unpack each snack. I can't help but smile at how concentrated he is.

"Do you think this will be enough?" He looks up at me, waiting for me to answer.

"Oh, um, yeah. This is more than enough," I say as I stare at the abundance of snacks that I know we aren't going to finish on our own.

We carry them into the living room and dump them on to the coffee table before settling on to the couch. At first, I'm not sure how to sit and, from the look on Blake's face, he isn't either. Sure, we've watched movies together but it was never just us. The girls were always around somewhere, and now that Blake and I are finally completely alone, it all feels so new.

We both decide to just sit down how we normally sit. I grab the remote before pulling a blanket over our legs and resting my head on his shoulder. He wraps his arm around me, and I can't help the warmth that spreads throughout my body as it always does when I'm sitting so close to Blake. We are halfway through *Me Before You* when Blake gets up to use the bathroom. I pause the movie and check my phone, cursing under my breath when I see a text from Alison asking for advice on what to wear on her dinner date with Noah. Luckily, she ended up choosing the cutest outfit out of the three she sent.

I check a few of my notifications when suddenly my phone is snatched out of my hands. I turn to see Blake with a cheeky smile on his face as he opens my camera app and begins to flood my phone with selfies of him.

"You're going to use up my storage!" I groan as I rush off the couch and over to him. "Give it back!"

"Not until you say the magic word!" He laughs as he runs into the kitchen. I can hear the sound of my camera clicking several times, which tells me I am definitely going to have tons of photos to delete.

"Please?" I can't help but laugh at his childlike behavior as I follow him.

"Nope!" He manages to get away. I run after him, cutting through the living room until we reach the stairs.

"Blake Harper!" I narrow my eyes at him, climbing up the stairs. I follow him into my room and I see he is now sitting on my bed, still snapping photos of himself. A part of me wants to smile at how cute he is, but the other part of me is not looking forward to not having any space left on my phone.

"You are so annoying!" I roll my eyes as I stand in front of him and snatch my phone from his grasp.

"Aw, come on! Don't be mad!" I'm not mad at all. I just think it's cute to see him like this, and every day, it's like I discover new sides to him. I go into my photo gallery, trying my best not to smile at all the silly pictures.

I feel Blake's hands on my hips, and he pulls me towards him so that I'm standing in between his legs. He takes my phone from my hands and sets it down next to him on the bed before his eyes focus on me. It's difficult not to blush under Blake's stare; his ocean eyes make me feel naked, as if he's seeing the parts of me I don't let anyone see.

We begin to inch closer until our lips are brushing against each other, and it's impossible to keep myself from connecting them. So I do. His lips move against mine, almost rhythmically, and neither of us seem to make an effort to stop it. Blake proceeds to lean back on to my bed and I find myself crawling on to it as well, straddling my legs over his waist. We don't break the kiss as his hands graze up and down my waist, tightening their grip around them. Things are quickly getting heated and a sudden feeling of fear begins to arise. I'm not used to doing things like this, and the last thing I want to do is make a fool out of myself or let it get too far. Those feelings begin to fade as my hands move under Blake's hoodie, feeling his abdomen, which is almost sizzling.

A gasp escapes me when Blake suddenly flips us over, using his arms to hover himself over me. For what seems like the hundredth time since we've started dating, I can't seem to get enough of the enigma who is Blake Harper. He is addicting in every way possible and being with him is something I wish I could spend forever doing.

"Alexa," he says, breaking our kiss and sitting up on the bed.

"What's wrong?" I prop myself up on my elbows to look up at him. His face is flustered, his hair is disheveled, and his lips are plump and red.

"Wait here." He stands from the bed and walks out the door. I hear him jog down the stairs, and a few seconds later, he is jogging back up until he is in the room again.

"What's that?" I ask, referring to the small box in his hands. There's now a smile on his face and he makes his way over to me.

"For a while now . . ." He pauses, taking a deep breath. "I've been wanting to say something and I just haven't built up the courage until now."

He places the box in my hands. I open it, revealing the most gorgeous sterling silver necklace. From it hangs a pendant in the shape of a heart. I'm so busy admiring the piece of jewelry that I almost miss the words that come out of Blake's mouth.

"I love you, Alexa Parker." His eyes are staring straight into mine and the familiar warm feeling begins to buzz through me, only this time, stronger than ever. The butterflies in my stomach are flapping with full force and I find myself unable to respond from every sensation I'm feeling.

"You don't have to say it back if you're not ready yet, but I just wanted you to know—"

Before he can say anything else, I pull him towards me again as I press my lips on to his and cut off his rambling. He relaxes and kisses back, smiling against my lips. When I pull back, his eyes are still closed. My heart drums as I say the words I've been wanting to say for a while too.

"I love you, Blake Harper."

CHAPTER TWENTY-EIGHT

Turning in my college application is terrifying. Even more so because everyone already seems to have turned theirs in, and some are already hearing decisions about their college applications. Unlike the Harpers who've been working on theirs for months, I've only started working on mine a couple of weeks ago.

The more I think about it, the more worried I get. New York University is one of the top schools in the United States, and I'm turning in an application that I only started working on a few weeks ago. Sure, I was able to return to getting straight A's and, as of now, I'm number three in my class, but what if that isn't good enough? What if they can see straight through my application and see the girl who was ready to completely throw her life away just a few months ago?

NYU's overall acceptance rate for twenty-eighteen is sixteen percent, and my chances of getting in are slim. I didn't even apply to a safety school. What kind of person doesn't even have a safety school? I am so screwed. I need to stop thinking like this. I need to prepare myself for the possibility that I may not get into NYU, and if I don't, I will figure something out. At least I hope so.

"Alexa, get down here and help me set the table!" my mother yells from downstairs.

I sigh as I give myself a quick look in the mirror and make my way downstairs.

Last week, Blake told me that he loved me.

Last week, I told Blake that I loved him too.

It's all I can think about, and each time I think about it, my heart swells with happiness.

"Go get the glasses from in the kitchen," my mom says frantically when she sees me.

"Quick, they'll be here any minute."

By 'they', she means the Harpers. My mother kept her promise when she said that the Harpers will be invited over for dinner, and though I'm happy that I will get to see Blake, I'm dreading the inevitable awkwardness of the questions that will be asked. My dad walks in while fixing his cuffs and helps me carry all the glasses into the dining room when he sees me struggling.

"Please don't try to scare him," I say to him.

"No promises," he replies, and as if on cue, the doorbell rings.

I look at my mom and then my dad before we all rush to the door. My mom fixes her hair and I smooth down my dress before she opens the door. The Harpers are standing there with huge smiles on their faces, and I ignore my nerves and give them a smile of my own. My eyes travel over Mrs. and Mr. Harper, then Alison and Madison and then Blake. My heart flutters at the way he looks at me, and I want nothing more than to kiss him . . but I can't. Not with everyone around us.

"Amanda! David! Thank you so much for coming," my mother greets as she lets them in.

"Thank you for having us!" Mrs. Harper replies as she pulls my mother in for a hug while my dad and Mr. Harper shake hands.

"Hey!" Alison hugs me, Madison doing the same after. Blake steps in front of me with a smile on his face and I take in how good he looks today.

Who am I kidding? He looks good every day.

If there's anyone who can make a plain black pair of jeans and a grey long-sleeved tee look good, it's Blake.

"Hi," he says.

I wrap my arms around his torso and pull him in for a hug. I can feel our parents watching us and my face heats up as he pulls away.

"Well," my mother starts. "I hope you guys like Italian!"

*   *   *

The dinner isn't as awkward as I thought it will be, and Blake and I aren't bombarded with questions about our relationship. It seems that our parents have come to some mutual agreement not to embarrass us tonight and I'm thankful for that. Blake compliments my mom on how amazing the food tastes, and I can tell that she's already in love with him. My dad, on the other hand, is a little more difficult to read.

"So, Alexa," Mr. Harper starts. "What are your plans for college?"

Everyone looks at me expectantly and I clear my throat.

"Oh, well, I actually just sent in an application for New York University."

"Really?" Mrs. Harper's eyes visibly light up. "What do you plan on studying?"

"Journalism," I say.

"I graduated from NYU. I could write you a recommendation!" Mrs. Harper says and my eyes widen.

"Really? You'd do that?" I ask, my heart starting to thump faster from excitement.

"Of course."

And just like that, my fears about not getting into NYU disappear. A recommendation from a notable alumni to any university is like a golden ticket and could play a very big role in my acceptance.

"Thank you so much!" My excitement is now at an all-time high and I consider getting up to engulf her in a tight hug or maybe even kiss her feet, but that would be doing too much.

"What about you, Blake? What are your plans?" my dad asks as he takes a sip of his wine.

"I want to go to Stanford and study law, sir," Blake replies, and I don't miss the hint of surprise and respect in my dad's eyes.

"Wow, Stanford," my dad says. "Think you'll get in?"

"I hope so," Blake replies.

My hand interlocks with his under the table and I give it a squeeze. Alison and Madison talk about how they want to go to the Fashion Institute of Technology. We gush about how if everything goes according to plan, both of our universities will be in New York and less than twenty minutes away from each other.

My mom brings out gelato for dessert. Shortly after helping clean up, I find myself in my backyard laying in the grass with the Harper triplets, competing to see who could find the most constellations.

"Oh! There's the big dipper," Alison exclaims.

"And there's the little dipper under it," Madison adds.

"Those are the easiest to find," I say.

"Then why didn't you point them out first?" Alison counters.

"Because those are the obvious ones." I laugh.

"Whatever," she says as she laughs too.

We go back to searching for more constellations, and I can't help but think about all the times Cam and I used to do this. We went through an astronomy phase freshman year and would spend hours researching galaxies and stars.

"Did you know you could buy a star?" Cam asks.

"No," I reply as I look up from my laptop screen.

"Apparently, you can buy a star and name it."

"Sounds like an amazing gift idea," I say.

"We should buy one," she starts. "And it can symbolize our friendship."

"And we can name it Camlexa!" I say excitedly.

One of the many things we never got to do.

I blink away the tears and push all the sad thoughts to the back of my mind. I focus on the night sky and search the stars for any hidden figures.

"There's Orion the Hunter." Blake points towards the left. I easily make out the figure, wishing that I found it first.

"How are you finding these? I've never even heard of that one," Madison says as she squints to where Blake is pointing.

"I think I remember hearing a story about it one time," Alison says.

"I think that's enough stargazing for me," Madison concludes.

The rest of us agree and make our way back inside.

"Wait," Blake says as he grabs my hand and pulls me into him.

"What are you doing?" I laugh.

"Something I can't exactly do in front of our parents." His hands cup my face and our lips meet for a kiss. *I wish I don't have to pull away.*

"We should join everyone before they come searching for us," I say.

"Yeah, we should," he says but neither of us move.

We stay exactly as we are with his hands cupping my face, our foreheads resting together, noses touching. We're standing so close together that I can feel the rhythm of his heartbeat.

"I love you," I say because I can and because I really and truly love Blake Harper. I say it because I know he feels the same way.

"I love you." He doesn't just say it; he declares it. My heart swells so much that it feels like it might burst.

If someone had told me months ago that I would love someone the way I loved Blake in a matter of a few months, I would have scoffed in their face. Because never would I have thought that someone will be able to mend my broken and jagged pieces like Blake has.

"We should really go now before they get suspicious." I laugh as I pull away.

He pecks me on the lips one more time before interlacing our fingers. Together, we walk into the living room where everyone is laughing at something my dad has said. They all look at us as Blake and I walk in together. I grow embarrassed at my mom's raised eyebrows and at the way everyone is looking at our interlocked hands.

"Hmm," she hums. "Now, I wonder what you guys were up to."

CHAPTER TWENTY-NINE

There are quite a few things I wish someone told me before starting high school.

One, popularity isn't everything.

Two, not everyone is your friend.

And three, cherish the friends you have before they're gone.

I wish I had known these things before starting high school, because maybe if I had, things won't be the way they are now. If I had known these things, I would have been more observant. I wouldn't have been some oblivious teen who lets everything get by her.

If I had known these things, Cam would probably still be here.

I play with the necklace Blake gave me on Valentine's Day and bury my head in my locker. Blake had to go turn in his lacrosse uniform since the season is over, so he won't be able to walk me to class. The bell rings and I sigh before shutting my locker, not bothering to take out any books. We are well into April, and today is the day of the annual pep rally they hold for all seniors. It's supposed to be an all-day thing filled with fun activities and performances.

It's something that Cam and I have always looked forward to experiencing when we were finally seniors. And now that it's happening, she isn't here to experience it. Alison and Madison wait for me by their lockers, and together, we walk to our homeroom class.

"Okay," Ms. Anderson starts, waiting for the noise to stop. "In about five minutes, you all will be heading down to the gym for the senior pep rally. If you have your bags with you, feel free to leave them in my class as you won't have any use for them during the day. Any questions?" We all shake our heads to signal that we don't have any questions.

"Alright then. You guys can head to the gym," she says.

The girls and I stay at the end of the line as we follow the rest of the students down to the gym. I've never realized how many seniors there are until now that we are all grouped together.

It's nowhere near the size of this year's freshmen class, but it's still a sizable class.

As we're divided into groups for the activities, I see one of the doors to the gymnasium open and in walks Blake along with Elliot, one of his friends from the lacrosse team. Blake laughs at something he says before his eyes scan the room, almost automatically finding mine.

I find it crazy how we can do that. It's like we are naturally drawn to each other. A smirk grows on his lips as his eyes remain locked on mine, but before he can walk over to me, he is picked by one of the teachers for the game of tug of war. We give each other a we'll-talk-later look. I turn back to my team who is already receiving directions from the teachers.

"For this activity, you will be divided into pairs that we will pick." Mrs. Himely, the counselor, chirps. I groan, noticing that I have no friends in this group whatsoever. Everyone begins to move around as they call up the pairs, and when there are only six of us left, I finally get called.

"Alexa," she calls me before looking down at her clipboard. "And Matt."

A feeling of dread falls over me as I turn to look at Matt who sheepishly steps forward. We make our way towards the other pairs, neither of us saying a word. I'm sure he's just as upset with the arrangement as I am, but instead of being difficult, we both suck it up for the sake of the rally. We are told that we will be competing against the other pairs in an ultimate fort-contest and it instantly lifts my mood. Looks like all of those nice building forts with Caleb and Braden as children will finally pay off. Once we learn that we will only have ten minutes to build the fort, I quickly begin planning it out.

"I can make the base if you want," Matt speaks up for the first time. He looks unsure of his own words.

"Um, yeah . . . that'd help a lot." He gives me a nod before heading towards the supply tables.

"Two minutes!" Mrs. Himely yells after some time, and I high five Matt as we both proudly stand next to our finished fort. Believe it or not, working with Matt isn't the worst thing ever. Or maybe I'm just too focused on what I'm doing to think about what he's done.

"Alexa," he calls out to me as I snap pictures of the fort. I hum in response, looking around the area at the other pairs who are close to finishing.

"I'm sorry." I don't need to ask to know what he's referring to. "I know you blame me, and I've been blaming myself, too, but I did love her and if I would've known—"

He doesn't get to finish his apology because we suddenly hear a commotion on the other side of the gymnasium.

It doesn't take me long to find Blake at the center of it, having an intense stare off with Julian. My heartbeat quickens in worry, and I don't hesitate to march over there, trying to see what's going on. Julian's eyes land on me and the sinister smirk on his face grows.

"Alexa, we were just talking about you." He turns to Blake. "Blake was telling me about how freaky girls like you are in bed, right, Blake?" I roll my eyes, knowing he's just making this up in an attempt to get a rise out of Blake.

"Julian, shut the—" Blake starts.

"Make me!" he yells. That's all it takes to make Blake lose control. He marches over to him and swings at his jaw, knocking Julian off his feet.

"Blake, stop it!" I yell at him, surprised that no administrators have noticed what's going on. Elliot is quick to take action and pull Blake away from Julian. The look on Blake's face sends shivers down my spine and I know that he's livid.

He turns to Julian who is still on the ground with blood oozing out of his nose. Despite his condition, he manages to laugh. It's one of those laughs that the antagonists have in movies—the kind of laugh that makes you uncomfortable and scared for what happens next.

"You better watch your back, Harper," Julian warns as one of the guys on his team helps him up. Blake narrows his eyes at him, not seeming threatened in the least.

"Miller!" the gym coach calls out to Julian. "What happened?"

"He fell," Elliot steps in. "I guess that tug of war match got pretty intense, huh?"

Caleb doesn't make a move to get Blake in trouble. The gym coach looks between Julian and Blake, but instead of saying anything, he shrugs it off seemingly deciding that digging deeper into the situation isn't worth the trouble.

"Are you okay?" I turn to Blake with concern evident in my eyes. Fortunately, Julian didn't hit him back, which proves he was intentionally trying to get a rise out of Blake, waiting for him to snap.

"I'm okay," he says as he takes my hands in his. "And I'm sorry, I know I shouldn't have reacted but I couldn't just let him say those things—" I press my lips against his, stopping his words.

"I know," I breathe out when I pull away. "But you could've gotten in trouble."

"It would be worth it, knowing I got to shut Julian up." I shake my head at him.

"I have to go back to my side now," I tell him. He groans as he wraps his arms around me, not letting me out of his grasp. I laugh and a part of me wishes we could ditch this rally.

"Come over after school?" I ask.

"Of course." He grins at me.

"Alright, see you then." He gives me one last kiss before we go our separate ways. As I walk back, I turn to him seeing that his eyes are still on me. He winks at me and my heart flutters at the small action. This boy will be the death of me.

When I get back to my station, I see Matt with a wide smile on his face as he holds up two first-place ribbons.

"Good job, Parker." He smiles. I know that he's still a bit unsure about how to act around me.

"I forgive you, Matt." I sigh and his eyes light up at my words.

I know that it isn't right to hold Matt accountable for Cam's death. No matter how much I wanted to blame someone, Matt isn't the person to blame. Cam had a lot more going on than she was willing to share, and Matt was just a factor. I believe him when he says he loved Cam. I need to move on from what happened, and I can't do that if I'm still blaming someone for her death. In order for me to live in peace, I need to forgive. So I forgive; I forgive Matt and it feels like a weight is lifted off of my chest.

CHAPTER THIRTY

April soon turned into May, and before I know it, it's finals week. I spent the last few weeks studying rigorously and checking my mail twice a day for any letter from NYU. This past month, to say the least, has been very stressful. I take a sip of my coffee as I walk to my locker, trying to blink the sleep out of my eyes. Today is the last day of finals, and I want nothing more than for it to be over already.

I squint at the flyer taped on to my locker with the word 'PROM' in bulky font. With everything going on, it slipped my mind that prom is this Saturday and, to be honest, I haven't put much thought into whether I want to go or not. It isn't something that Blake and I have talked about either, despite the fact that we've witnessed at least twenty promposals this week.

Speaking of Blake, I haven't seen him at all this morning. He usually always meets me at my locker. I grab what I need and put away what I don't need before shutting my locker and heading to the hallway where the girls' lockers are. I spot them talking to Blake and my heart flutters when I see him.

"Hey," I greet and they abruptly stop talking. The girls smile at me in response. Blake's mouth lifts into a half-smile and not the blinding smile he always gives me.

"Did I miss something?" I question.

"Nope," Alison and Madison reply at the same time.

"I have to go," Blake says. "I'll see you, guys, later." He barely looks at me as he walks away and my brows furrow in confusion.

"Seriously, did I miss something?" I ask again, baffled by the way Blake is acting.

"Maybe he's just stressed about finals," Alison says.

"Yeah, maybe," I mutter as the bell rings.

On the way to class, I can't help the number of thoughts racing through my mind. *Did I do something wrong? Is Blake getting tired of me? Has he finally realized that I come with more than he's bargained for?* My heart drops at the last two thoughts.

"I'm sure it's nothing," Madison says, seemingly sensing my thoughts.

We take our seats and our teacher immediately tells us to put our things away and get ready for our exam. I try to focus as much as I can, but with thoughts of Blake plaguing my mind, it's nearly impossible to concentrate. I somehow finish before time is called and pray that I did well when our teacher comes around to collect our papers.

I part ways with Alison and Madison, agreeing to meet them at lunch before heading off to my next class to take my second final exam of the day. When lunch finally comes around, I can't be more relieved. I have one more final after this and then this stressful week can finally come to an end.

"We should go out after school," Madison starts as I join them at our table outside. "Treat ourselves to some ice cream or something for getting through finals week."

"I'm down," Alison replies.

"Sounds great," I say.

I'm still thinking about Blake, and the fact that he hasn't shown up for lunch does nothing to calm my nerves. I decide not to ask the girls if they know where he is. All my worries cause my appetite to vanish, and I end up tossing the remainder of my lunch away. Lunch goes by quickly and I find myself in my AP Calculus class with my phone in hand as I stare at all my unanswered messages to Blake. He's being really weird. The longer I think about it, the more I start to think that I'm the problem, and the more I think about that, the more I want to cry.

This is exactly what I'm afraid of. I know it's only a matter of time before Blake realizes that we aren't good for each other, and the fact that I still let myself fall for him adds salt to the wound.

"Please put everything away so that we may begin the exam," my teachers says. I shut my phone off before shoving it into my bag.

I try to push all thoughts of Blake to the back of my mind as she starts to hand out the exam papers. I can't afford to fail my final over this, and no matter how much I just want to break down and cry, now isn't the time nor place. When the bell rings an hour and a half later and the exams have been collected, I couldn't have gotten out of that classroom faster. I fish my keys out of my bag while pushing my way through the crowd of students crowding in the parking lot.

Cheers erupt through the crowd as we have, yet again, another promposal.

"There you are!" Alison says excitedly as she sees me approaching. She and Madison are standing by my car waiting for me.

"Guys," I start. "I'm not really in the mood to do anything right now."

"Oh, come on!" Madison protests. "I've been looking forward to getting ice cream all day."

"You can still get ice cream without me."

"The idea was for all three of us to go." She pouts.

"Besides," Alison says. "Blake was our ride to school and he had to leave early so you're kind of stuck with us."

"Do you know where he went? I haven't seen him all day," I ask, my heart beating faster and a lump forming at the back of my throat at the mention of him.

"He didn't say," she replies. "But we are not going to let you go home just to worry about him, so get in the car so we can treat ourselves to ice cream."

All I want to do is go home but I know she's right. If I go home, I will think about Blake and how weird he's been acting today and how he hasn't answered any of my messages. I don't want to put myself through that. So I get in the car and drive to the nearest ice cream parlor. Alison and Madison belt out the lyrics of whatever song is on the whole car ride, and I have to admit that it does cheer me up a little. When we get to the parlor, Madison orders four scoops of fudge brownie ice cream. Alison and I share a look, knowing she won't finish it.

Alison orders two scoops of vanilla and I order one scoop of mint chocolate chip.

"Did you know that Caleb has a birthmark on his left butt cheek?" Madison asks casually as if it's the most normal thing to ask. Alison drops her spoon and I put my ice cream down. It doesn't look very appetizing at the moment.

"Why would we know that?" Alison says.

"Why do you know that?" I question, pressing the tips of my fingers to the temples of my head. "You know what? Don't answer that."

"Madison, seriously?" Alison whisper-yells as we all get up to throw our trash away.

"What?" Madison shrugs.

"Okay. I think we're done here. Time to go home," I say.

"Wait!" Alison exclaims as she checks her phone. "We can't go home."

"Why not?" I ask slowly, confusion evident on my face.

"Well, um, because the day's not over yet!" Madison replies quickly. "And we really want to go to the mall. Right, Alison?"

"Oh yeah, the mall!" Alison says.

I raise my eyebrows at how suspicious they are acting all of sudden.

"You guys seriously want to go to the mall?" I ask.

"Yes!" they reply simultaneously.

"PINK is having a sale and, uh, today's the last day. We can't miss it," Alison says.

I'm not an idiot. I know there's something they aren't telling me, and I have every reason to believe that Blake is somehow involved. Instead of calling them out, I agree to go to the mall with them and it just so happens that they weren't lying about the sale.

"Mads, it is seventy degrees outside. Do you really need five hoodies?" Alison stares at Madison as she hugs them in her arms.

"Quit acting like you won't be begging me to borrow these later on." Madison smirks.

"You have a point." Alison nods, turning back to the wall of different perfumes and body lotions.

"Alexa, aren't you going to at least look at something for yourself?" Madison pouts at me. I shrug, looking around.

When we get back to my house, the girls run up to my room and collapse on to my bed. As the two fill me in on their love lives, I find myself worrying about mine. Blake has yet to reply and I'm feeling worse by the second.

"Alexa." Alison stops Madison mid-sentence and the two turn to me. "You're crying. What's wrong?" I quickly wipe my tears and try to compose myself.

"I think Blake is tired of me." My voice cracks slightly and the two look at each other with concern on their faces. "He's been ignoring me all day, and I'm sure that it's because he's realized I'm too much for him."

"Alexa . . ." Madison walks over to me and hugs me, which just makes me cry even more.

A minute goes by and as my crying ceases, my phone begins to vibrate on my desk. Blake's name appears and I swipe my finger across the screen before bringing the phone up to my ear.

"Hey." I try my best to make my voice sound normal.

"Alexa, hey," he breathes through the phone. "I need to talk to you." My breathing ceases as those words leave his mouth, and if I could see my heart, I bet it will have the beginnings of a crack in it.

"About what?" The lump in my throat begins to feel unbearable.

"I'll explain when I see you. I'll be at your house in a bit, just meet me outside." He doesn't give me a chance to reply before he hangs up the phone.

"What did he say?" Alison asks.

"He said we need to talk." I choke out in between sobs. "He's going to break up with me."

"Alexa, he could've meant a number of things. I know my brother and I know he would never break up with you," Madison argues.

"He said to meet him outside." I ignore her attempt to get me to stop worrying. I get up from my chair, walking down the stairs and opening the front door, only to see Blake with his fist held up and about to knock.

He looks better than ever in his dark wash jeans and grey sweatshirt. The pain in my chest grows at the sight of him. The smile he gives me quickly turns into a look of worry as he examines my face.

"Babe, what happened? Were you crying?" His hands caress my cheeks as his eyes widen.

"If you're going to break up with me, just get it over with," I manage to say without crying. His eyebrows draw together in clear confusion.

"Woah." He takes a step back. "Why would you think I'm breaking up with you?" I can't describe the look on his face as he grabs my hand.

"Why else would you have been ignoring me all day?" I ask.

"I wasn't ignoring you." He looks into my eyes. "I was setting things up."

"Setting things up for what?" His face morphs into a smile as he grabs my hand and guides me down the steps of the porch towards my driveway. I see Alison and Madison standing on the driveway, holding up a large sheet, almost as if covering something from my view.

"Blake—" I am cut off when he suddenly turns around and plants a kiss on my lips. Those same sparks from the first time we've made an appearance, and I am left speechless when he pulls away.

"Alexa, I would never purposely ignore you," he assures me. "But the reason I was so absent today is because I was preparing this." He steps to the side and signals for the girls to move the sheet to reveal 'PROM?' spelled out in nothing but LED candles and rose petals.

Still processing what's happening, I take a step closer to admire the beauty of what Blake has put together. No one has ever gone through so much trouble to do something like this for me. I can't seem to find the words to express what I'm feeling. I feel Blake's arms circle around my waist, and I turn my head to see him already gazing at me. All I can do is smile.

"You like it?" he asks.

"I love it," I reply, still blown away by the gesture.

"So is that a yes?" He grins at me. I turn to look at him before pulling him in for a kiss.

When I pull away, I can feel some sort of humming electricity between us. My heart buzzes as I answer his question.

"Yes!" The girls' clapping pulls us out of our moment and I laugh at them, realizing that they are in on this the whole time.

"So this is why we couldn't come home earlier?" I raise an eyebrow.

I can't believe they let me cry like that to them moments ago.

"Obviously!" they both shriek before pulling me in for a group hug.

"We'll be inside if you need us." Madison grins as she makes her way up the driveway with Alison following closely behind.

When I turn to Blake, he's holding a bouquet of roses in his hands.

"You are just full of surprises, aren't you?" I smile.

"Actually, yes." He gives me a cheeky grin. "I still have one more surprise. Follow me."

He interlocks his fingers with mine and leads me through the gate to my backyard. At the center of the lawn is a white tent, and inside it are dozens of pillows and a pair of fuzzy blankets. As we get closer, I am hit with the smell of pizza. I step inside to see a picnic basket with a pizza box tied on top. Blake joins me in the tent and I turn to look at him even more amazed.

How did he pull all of this off?

"The telescope is so we can find the star I got you," he says.

"You got me a star?" My raises a few octaves to indicate my shock. He nods before handing me a photo frame with the certificate in it.

"This is why I had to leave school early." He pauses. "I had to make sure we would be able to see the star tonight."

This entire time, my heart has not stopped racing. Blake is truly amazing and I feel awful for ever doubting him.

"Blake, I'm so sorry I doubted you." I look down and he tilts my chin upward. His ocean eyes stare into mine before he kisses me gently and sweetly yet with such fervor that a warmth spreads throughout my body.

"Here," he says when we pull away. "Let's find your star."

It takes us a while to find it, but when we finally do, I swear it's the most beautiful thing I've ever seen.

"It's breathtaking, isn't it?" I ask as I adjust the telescope to get a better look at it.

"Yeah," he whispers, not once taking his eyes off of me. "It is."

CHAPTER THIRTY-ONE

Prom. The rite of passage for all high school students. I admire myself in front of the full-length mirror, doing a turn in the beautiful white floral dress the girls helped me pick out. My hair is loosely curled and cascades down my back in small ringlets.

"Wow," my mom breathes as she leans against the door frame. "You look beautiful." Her eyes start to water and I smile as I pull her in for a hug.

"Thanks, Mom." I inhale the scent of her flowery perfume as I try not to shed some tears of my own.

"Blake is downstairs waiting," she says when we pull away. "You are going to render him speechless in that dress." I take a nervous breath as I grab my clutch and give myself one more look in the mirror before following my mom downstairs.

Blake is having a conversation with my dad when I get down. At first, he doesn't see me, but when my dad clears his throat as he looks at me, Blake follows his line of sight. He's exactly what my mom said he would be; he's rendered speechless. He stares at me in awe and his pupils dilate. He tries to say something but no words come out. I can feel my face heat up as I take the last few steps down the stairs and make my way over to him, careful not to trip.

"You . . ." he says. "Look absolutely stunning."

My face heats up even more, knowing that my parents are watching us.

"You don't look so bad yourself," I reply.

He looks like he wants nothing more than to kiss me and, trust me, I want nothing more than to do the same, but with my parents around, we're forced to restrain ourselves.

"Let's take a picture before you, guys, go!" my mom exclaims as she gets out her phone camera.

Blake and I pose for what has to be about one hundred photos before we finally get out of the house and into Blake's jeep. Alison and Madison aren't riding with us since they're getting picked up by their own dates, but we all promised to meet up as soon as we arrive at the venue where my school chose to have the prom. I notice Blake staring at me every once in a while and I try not to laugh as I turn to him.

"Eyes on the road, mister!" I scold.

"It's hard to concentrate when you're sitting next to me, looking so beautiful." He smirks as my cheeks turn noticeably red. It's still hard to receive compliments from him without blushing.

"Well, try! I'd like to get to prom without any accidents." He laughs as the hand he's not using to drive interlocks with mine. I can't help the butterflies that always appear whenever I'm around Blake.

We spend the rest of the drive in comfortable silence. When I see Alison and Madison standing in the parking lot with their dates, I nearly jump in my seat with excitement as Blake rushes over to open the door for me. They squeal as they walk over as fast as they can in their heels.

"You, guys, look amazing!" I say as they both do a spin in their dresses.

"So do you!" Alison replies.

"That dress is made for you," Madison says.

The guys do their weird handshake thing and then we're all walking into the venue together. The inside is beautiful; it looks like they decided to go with some type of heavenly theme because the entire room is decorated in white and gold with fairy lights throughout the room and clouds hanging from the ceiling.

There are people taking pictures and some sitting at tables, sipping from flutes of sparkling water. Most people are on the dance floor, dancing to some upbeat song. We decide to grab a table before they're all taken, and the girls and I leave the boys to watch our bags as we make our way to the photo booth to take pictures while the night is still young rather than at the end of the night when we will no doubt look like hot messes.

"I'm really glad we're here together," I say to them, reflecting on how far I've come from a few months ago.

If it weren't for them sitting at my lunch table all those months ago after Cam's death, then I probably won't even be here tonight. I will probably be at home, the same numb and bitter teenage girl watching her life crumble right in front of her, and not doing anything about it.

"Me too," they say simultaneously, pulling me in for a group hug.

"Come on," Alison starts when we pull away. "Let's get out of here and dance with our boyfriends before we start getting all sappy."

When we get back to our table, the boys look like they're having a serious conversation, but their eyes light up when they see us. A slow song comes on and Alison and Madison lead Noah and Caleb away until it's just Blake and me.

"May I have this dance?" I ask as I extend my hand out to him.

"You may." He grabs on to my hand and I lead him to the dance floor.

He circles his arms around my waist and pulls me in close as I wrap my arms around his neck, resting my head against his chest.

"I can't get over how beautiful you are," he says as we sway to the music. I look up at him, cupping his face in my hands and pull him in for a kiss. The song ends as we pull away and changes to something upbeat again.

"Alexa, I have to tell you something," he says, his face getting serious.

"Alexa, we have to dance. This is our song!" Madison appears out of nowhere and starts pulling me away.

"Tell me later!" I yell out to him before I'm engulfed in a sea of people and can't see him anymore.

We somehow end up dancing to a few more songs, and by the time we detach from the crowd, we are sweaty and out of breath. When I look back at the table, I don't see Blake. I scan the room and spot him at the refreshments table, sipping on water. A pang of guilt hits me as I realize I haven't really been with him at all tonight.

"Hey," I say sheepishly.

"Hey." He puts his glass down and I move to stand in front of him.

"Sorry we haven't had much time together tonight. It's supposed to be our night." I pout.

"Do you want to go outside where it's less stifling?" he asks and I nod.

It's starting to get really hot in here, and some fresh air is exactly what I need right now. Outside, the night air is chilly and there isn't a cloud in the sky. Only the beautiful expanse of the darkness and the millions of stars it holds. I try looking for the star Blake had gotten me, but I know it's pointless without the telescope. Blake wraps his arms around me from behind me and I lean into him. Tonight is perfect. It's everything that I hope it will be, and though I didn't get to spend much of it with Blake, it doesn't matter because we will have the rest of the night together.

"I have to tell you something," he says and I look up at him, confused by the weird look on his face.

"What is it?" I ask.

"I got into Stanford," he says.

"That's amazing! I had no doubt you wouldn't get in! I'm so happy for you," I say with a giant smile forming on my face. That smile falters when I notice that he doesn't look that excited.

"Aren't you happy? Blake, you got into freakin' Stanford!"

"Believe me, I'm happy." He tries to give me a smile but it doesn't meet his eyes.

"So why do you look like that?" I reach my arm out to grab his hand and he sighs.

"Alexa, Stanford is in California."

"Okay . . ." I say, still a little confused at what exactly he's trying to say.

Then it hits me.

If Blake goes to Stanford, then that means he will be on the other side of the world. We will end up becoming one of those couples who try to make a long distance relationship work, when we both know long distance relationships rarely work. He will be too busy trying to get through law school that we will never have time to talk. We will be one of those long distance couples who inevitably break up. I look at him and take a step back as my heart starts to beat faster.

"Are you going to go?" I ask, my voice cracking.

His silence is answer enough. That was a stupid question; of course, he's going to go. Stanford is a freaking Ivy League, one of the top schools in the entire world, and he will be stupid to pass up an opportunity like that. Even for me. I put my hand over my mouth to keep the sob from escaping.

"Alexa." He reaches out to me but I take another step back.

"We were never supposed to work, were we?" My vision is blurry and I know that the tears are going to fall. "You knew that you were going to have to end up leaving me yet you still let me fall in love with you."

"Alexa, how could you say that?" His voice falters as he looks me straight in the eyes. I can see the pain in his ocean eyes— like the roiling of waves during a storm.

"It's true." My sadness has slowly become anger, and I don't care about how ridiculous I sound right now. I feel like all the progress I've made these last few months is regressing.

"Are you hearing yourself?" He scoffs at me in pure incredulity. "Do you think I planned for this to happen, Alexa?" The volume of his voice is now higher than before.

"This entire time you've been with me, you could have talked to me about it instead of letting me live with the idea that you were never going to leave my side!" The tears are running down my face and I vigorously wipe at them.

"Don't you think this is hard for me too?" he yells back.

This time when I look at him, I see the tears brimming his eyes. He manages to keep the stability in his voice, but I can tell that it won't last much longer. "I fell in love too!" His voice cracks.

"But you—" I start.

"No, listen to me!" he snaps. "This is hurting me, too, Alexa. The thought of me leaving and not being able to see you every day is killing me, and for you to think that I wanted this to happen is hurting me even more!" He grabs on to my hand but I yank it out of his grasp.

"Just . . . stop," I say in between sobs as I continue to stagger back.

It all hurts too much and I can't breathe. This is exactly what I'm afraid will happen . . . that I will let someone in and they will end up leaving me just like Cam did.

"Alexa, please," he begs.

There's the sound of the doors to the venue opening. When I look up, I see Madison, Alison, and Caleb with bewildered looks on their faces. I start to walk away and he calls out after me.

"At least let me take you home." I can hear his footsteps behind me but I don't turn around. "We need to talk about this."

"No," I say, not able to bear the thought of being in a car with him because I know I won't be able to contain myself. "Caleb will take me home."

Caleb doesn't ask any questions as he follows me to his car. I look at the girls and the look in their eyes tells me that they know. As I walk to Caleb's car, I can hear Blake call my name one last time, but I don't look back as I walk away from the man I love, knowing that if I do, I won't be able to stop my heart from breaking anymore than it already has.

That's the thing with love. You become so dependent on your significant other—almost like they're a lifeline. And when that lifeline is ripped away from you, your heart doesn't just break.

It shatters.

CHAPTER THIRTY-TWO

Popularity. Drama. Fights. Losing my best friend. Losing myself. Heartbreak. If a few months or even years from now someone were to ask me what my high school experience was like, I would list all of those things.

Today is graduation day. A day that I looked forward to since my freshman year, but now that it's finally here, all I can feel is dread. I feel physically and emotionally drained and all I want to do is sleep, but I can't do that. Instead, I sit in front of my mirror and try my best to do my makeup and cover up the fact that I haven't slept in days. I haven't slept much since prom, which was a few days ago. I can't stop thinking about Blake. I miss him but the thought of seeing him and the thought of us having to go our separate ways hurts too much. I'm tired of hurting.

"Are you ready for your big day?" my father asks as he sticks his head through the door.

"As ready as I can be," I reply with a small smile.

"I'm proud of you, you know," he says as he walks over to me. "My only kid leaving me and going to NYU." His eyes start to water, which catches me off guard because it's a rare sight to see my dad cry.

"Come on, Dad. Don't cry or you'll make me cry." I pull him in for a hug and squeeze tight.

"I love you," he says.

"I love you too," I reply.

"Alexa, if we don't leave now, we'll be late! You don't want to be late to your own graduation, do you?" my mom calls from downstairs and my dad laughs as we pull away from our embrace.

"Your mother's right. We should really get going," he says as he makes his way to the door.

"I'll be down in a second." I wait for him to leave before turning to the mirror again and taking a deep breath.

Today, I'll be ending a chapter of my life and starting a new one. Today is one of the most important days of my life and I'm going to get through it. When I get to the school, the hallways are crammed with teens in their caps and gowns. I push my way through them and head to the gym where everyone is supposed to sign in.

"Name?" the lady asks when I walk up to the sign-in table.

"Alexa Parker," I say. She smiles at me as she checks my name off the list.

I turn around and start to walk off when I hear someone call my name. My body goes rigid as I turn around.

"Alexa, hey!" Madison calls as she pushes her way through a group of people with Alison following behind her.

"Hey," I reply with my eyes searching.

"You can relax," Alison starts. "Just because you're avoiding Blake doesn't mean you have to avoid us too."

"I know. I'm sorry." I sigh. "W-where is he?"

"We told him to give you some space. He's a mess, Alexa. He wants to see you," Madison replies.

"You should at least see him before you leave today," Alison adds.

Before I can formulate a response, someone announces over the loudspeakers that it is now time for us to move to the auditorium so that we can all be seated before the parents are ushered in.

The girls and I go our separate ways since we'll be seated alphabetically by last name, which I'm thankful for because it means that I don't have to face Blake so soon. I know that I need to talk to him. It's inevitable. Just not today. I need today to be a good day. We all pile into the auditorium, and once everyone is seated, they open the doors for our parents and loved ones. I watch as our principal, Mrs. Frey, walks up to the podium to start her commencing speech.

"I want to welcome you all to the class of twenty-eighteen graduation ceremony," she starts. "I would like to take the opportunity to congratulate our soon-to-be former students on the completion of your high school education. I am extremely proud of every single one of you, and though it will be sad to see you all go, this should be an extremely happy moment for all of us."

I zone out for most of the speech but start to pay attention towards the end.

"Today, you will be ending one phase of your life and moving on to the next one. I can't wait to see what the future holds for all of you. Before we begin the awarding of diplomas, I'd like to take a moment of silence for a student that left us too soon. Cameron Smith."

My body goes rigid at the sound of her name and a picture of her appears on the screen. I didn't know they were going to do this. Where did they even get that picture of her? I notice a few heads turn to look at me, expecting a reaction, but I just stare straight ahead as I keep my face void of any emotion. I expect the tears to come, but surprisingly, they don't. The room is completely silent for a few seconds and then the principal starts to talk again.

"Now, we'd like to begin the awarding of diplomas. Tyler Adams," she calls out and everyone claps as he walks on to the stage.

I start to zone out again after she calls about twenty names, but my ears perk up when I hear the last name, Harper.

"Alison Harper." I smile as Alison practically runs across the stage.

"Blake Harper." My breath catches when he walks on to the stage.

I haven't seen him since that night, and seeing him now in his cap and gown, makes my heart ache. He smiles as he receives his diploma, but even from where I'm sitting, I can see it doesn't meet his eyes. And then he's walking off the stage and Madison's name is called. When my name is called, I grow nervous and pray that I don't trip and fall in front of everyone in this room.

"Congratulations," Mrs. Frey says as I shake her hand and hold on to my diploma.

"Thank you," I say. I quickly shake everyone else's hands before making my way off the stage.

I sigh in relief as I make my way back to my seat. I fiddle with my diploma and drown out everything around me. Today is my graduation day. I should be ecstatic right now, and instead here I am, wishing that this day will just come to an end already.

"And now," Mrs. Frey starts, "a closing speech from our class valedictorian, Blake Harper." Everyone erupts into applause.

Then there he is, standing at the podium with a nervous smile on his lips as he struggles to remain still. His shaky hands flip through his note cards. He clears his throat before commencing his speech.

"To the administrators, officials, and peers here today, it is an honor to be giving this speech as valedictorian of the class of twenty-eighteen." After a short round of applause, he continues.

"In middle school, they tried their best to prepare us for what we have endured these last four years. Unfortunately, what those teachers failed to realize is that there is no amount of preparation that can make you completely ready to take on what high school has to offer. Though I haven't been here for all four years, this last year has been filled with moments of pure bliss as well as the opposite. We've partied at our sports games, but we've also shed our fair share of tears together during finals week." The crowd breaks out in laughter at his joke and I fail to keep a straight face.

"But throughout all the good and bad, I have realized that I would never trade these years of high school for anything. I wouldn't trade the inspiring teachers I've had the honor of meeting nor the loyal friends I've managed to make. They say that those you meet in high school aren't the ones that will stick, but I can not disagree more. High school has granted me the chance of meeting some of the most important people in my life. Those who have believed in me." His eyes are focused solely on me when he says those words, and I know that I'm not the only one who notices.

"Every day, we have a chance to believe in someone." He looks at me. "A chance to learn from someone, a chance to love someone. And it's that someone we love who wakes that passion inside of us. The passion to succeed." My heartbeat quickens and the emotions are becoming overwhelming.

"My only piece of advice to you, fellow classmates, is to find those people or that someone," he says. "Find the people who will only push you to try harder every day and will never allow you to quit. Find that someone who will bring out the best version of you, and most importantly, hold on to them forever."

Then, every emotion I've been holding in all week comes rushing at me. My heart starts to beat faster and faster. I drown out the noise of everyone clapping and cheering around me as they move the tassels of their caps to the other side to signify that we have officially graduated. I don't even notice that people are throwing their caps into the air until one lands on the floor at my feet. *I need to get out of here.* I can't bear to be in this stifling gown any longer. I push my way through groups of people until I find my parents.

"I can't believe my baby is officially done with high school," my mother says as she engulfs me into a tight hug.

"Proud of you, kiddo," my dad joins in.

"I'm ready to leave now," I say.

"What? Don't you want to take pictures?" my mother asks.

"Mom, can we please leave?" She must finally see the look in my eyes and the fact that I am on the verge of a panic attack because she just nods and grabs on to my hand as she leads me out of the overcrowded auditorium.

"This isn't about Blake, is it?" she asks me once we're in the parking lot.

She doesn't know exactly what happened the night of prom but she knows something happened. She's probably also figured out that Blake was talking about me in his speech. My silence is answer enough, and she doesn't say anything else the whole car ride home. When I get to my room, I check my phone to see messages from Alison and Madison.

Alison: Alexa, did you seriously already leave? We didn't even get to take our pictures.

Madison: I get that you're avoiding Blake but seriously???

Alison: You need to talk to him.

Madison: He knows you're leaving today.

Alison: Call us before you leave, please.

I don't reply to any of their messages and throw my phone on to my bed. The day after prom, my mom came into my room with my acceptance letter from NYU. I was ecstatic, but then it's like it doesn't even matter that I got in if I can't celebrate the news with the person I wanted to tell first. Though he probably found out about my acceptance the same day because my mother called Mrs. Harper immediately to thank her for writing me the letter of recommendation that likely played a big part in my acceptance.

I know that I'm probably being irrational, and I know that I'm probably being selfish for expecting him to choose my future over his. I just can't handle another person leaving me like Cam did. So maybe it's better for me to leave first. Today, I will be leaving to attend the college of my dreams and moving into an apartment that I will be sharing with Alison and Madison. I'm not even as happy about it as I should be.

"Alexa . . . oh sweety," my mom says as she rushes into the room.

I don't realize I'm crying until the first sob rakes through my body. I try to form a sentence but she cuts me off before I can say anything.

"It's okay. You don't need to say anything." She moves my hair out of my face as I continue to cry.

"I love him, Mom," I finally manage to get out. "And it hurts so much."

"I don't know exactly what happened between you, guys, but I can guess. And if your love is as strong as I know it is, you, guys, will find a way."

"What if we can't find a way?" I ask.

"Blake loves you, Alexa. Love like that is hard to find at this age and it's not so easily given up on." A part of me knows she's right, but the other part of me—the broken and scarred part of me—doubts that there will ever be a happy ending for Blake and me.

CHAPTER THIRTY-THREE

I watch the street lights blur past me, my head resting against the car window. The drive to the airport is at most a half-hour drive but it feels much longer and ominous. My legs won't stop shaking, no matter how much I try to get them to still and the feeling in the bottom of my stomach makes me feel like I'm going to be sick. My mom looks back at me from the passenger seat and puts her hand on my leg to stop the shaking. The car comes to a stop, and I look around to see that we're in the airport parking lot.

"You girls ready?" my dad asks.

"No," I say. "I am so not ready."

"It's okay, Alexa. I'll be with you and I won't leave until you're settled and the girls are with you."

"I know. I just—" *I miss Blake.* I wish he were here. I wish I had just talked to him, and now, it's too late.

"What is it?" my dad prods and I shake my head.

"Nothing. Let's go." I push the car door open and ignore the look that my dad gives my mom.

They get out of the car and my dad pops the trunk to grab our suitcases. Our flight isn't for another hour and a half, but it's always best to arrive early. I grab on to my dad's hand and squeeze to calm myself. A blast of cool air hits me as we walk into the airport and make our way to the airline desk to check in. It takes about fifteen minutes for the lady at the front desk to check our documents before we're able to proceed to security.

"I love you," my dad says as he pulls me in for a tight hug. He unfortunately won't be coming with us so this is where we have to say our goodbyes. "You're going to do great things there, Alexa. I'm so proud of you."

I can tell he's trying to hold back some tears so I pull him in for another hug, this one a little bit longer than the first one.

"I love you too," I whisper as I take in his signature scent of leather and vanilla one more time.

I turn my head as he pulls my mom in for a kiss. We watch as he walks away until we can't see him anymore. My mom and I make our way to security, which is a very long process. There's twenty minutes left until our flight when we get through security, so my mom and I start to head to our gate. I check my phone to see a message from Alison asking what time my flight is and what gate. Not long after I reply, she calls.

"Hey," I say.

"Are you about to board your flight?" she asks quickly.

"No, I'm walking to my gate right now."

"Alexa, why didn't you at least say goodbye to Blake? Do you have any idea what you're putting him through right now?" she yells.

"I know," I reply. "And I'm sorry. I just thought leaving him would hurt less if I didn't have to say goodbye." My mom starts to walk a few steps ahead of me to give me some privacy but I know she can still hear me.

"I know you're a totally different person from who you were before Cam died, and I know that the thought of someone else leaving your life terrifies you but Blake loves you, okay? And a little distance isn't going to change that."

"It's too late, Alison," I say, my voice starting to wobble. "I'm leaving and it's too late." I hear Madison say something in the background before Alison comes back to the phone.

"Maybe it's not too late," she says and I furrow my brows.

"What do you mean?" I ask.

That's when I hear him. At first, I think I'm imagining it. That I've tricked myself into hearing things but then I see him. Blake Harper, the boy who makes me feel like I'm on top of the moon whenever we're together, is calling my name and pushing his way through crowds of people to get to me.

This isn't real, I think. *These things only happen in movies.*

But it must be real because my mom stares at him in shock, which must mean she sees him too. I drop my bags on to the floor as he gets closer, and before I know it, his hands are gently cupping my face and he's kissing me. My arms instinctively wrap around his neck like they've done so many times before and then I'm kissing him back. The familiar feeling of butterflies and electricity appear. I don't even care that people are probably watching and that my flight is going to board very soon. All I can think about is how much I've missed this. How much I've missed him. We pull away, our foreheads resting against each other and breathing heavy.

"Blake," I start.

"We don't have much time," he says. "So let me say this. I know the thought of us being apart is terrifying, trust me, I know. But, I love you, Alexa, and I will do whatever it takes to keep you. Even if I'm on the other side of the world."

"Blake, I—"

"I promised you that I will never let you go, so now, it's your turn. Promise me, Alexa. Say you won't let go." He wipes the tears from my eyes as he waits for my answer.

"Promise me," he pleads.

I lean up to press my lips against his one last time.

"I promise."

EPILOGUE

2 years later

The bell on the door of the coffee shops rings as I walk in. I sigh happily as the fireplace in the shop instantly spreads a warmth throughout my body compared to the bitter cold outside. It's winter here in New York, and though I've been living here for about two years, I'm still not used to how cold it gets.

"Hey, gorgeous," Charlie, the barista, greets as I walk up to the counter to order.

"Hi, Charles," I reply, knowing that he hates it when I call him by his full name. Charlie was the first person I met when I first moved to New York. I clumsily bumped into him the first time I came into this coffee shop, and I soon discovered that we were both taking the same literature course at NYU.

"The usual?" he asks.

"Actually, make that three large coffees with a ton of espresso," I reply.

"Sounds like you and the girls are pulling an all-nighter again." I pull out my card to pay for the drinks, but he shakes his head and gives me one of those smiles that have the girls at NYU falling out of their seats. "It's on the house."

"Thanks, Charlie," I say as he hands me the drinks in one of those cardboard trays.

He winks at me as I push my way through the door and thrust myself back into the cold night air. As I get into my Uber, I can't help but notice how beautiful the sky looks tonight. It's littered with thousands of stars, and as I stare at them, I think of Blake.

I've only seen him once in the time that I've lived here and that was about a year and a half ago. We try to talk as much as we can, whether it were phone calls or face times or texts, but as he got busier and busier with school, we didn't get to talk much. It breaks my heart to think that what I feared will happen to us, is actually happening. The only way I know what he is up to is when he sends me weekly updates but even those stopped coming. He is so focused on school and pre-law that he even skips out on holidays and visits back home.

We eventually decided to take a break. He even told me that he wouldn't hold it against me if I found happiness with someone else no matter how much it would hurt him, but I will never be one-hundred percent happy without Blake. I'm still madly and invariably in love with him, and I can only hope that his feelings for me have remained the same.

The Uber comes to a stop outside of the penthouse I share with Alison and Madison. I thank the driver before heading into the building. It's so cold outside that it's a wonder the drinks have managed to retain their heat. Once I get on to my floor, I pray that I don't drop the drinks as I try to put the keys into the lock.

"Coffee's here!" I yell as I set them on to the kitchen island.

I kick off my shoes and hang up my coat as Alison and Madison rush into the kitchen.

"You're seriously the best," Alison says as she takes a sip of her coffee and practically moans.

"I second that," Madison says.

"Courtesy of Charlie. They were on the house," I reply as I, too, take a sip of my coffee.

We move to the living room where a week's work of homework is scattered around the carpet.

"I was wondering," I start. "Have you guys heard from Blake recently?"

"We talked to him this morning, but it was barely a minute conversation before he was rushed off the phone," Madison replies.

"Oh," I say, trying to ignore the pang of sadness that hits me.

"But he may have mentioned something about how he misses you and feels really guilty that things aren't the same between you, guys," she adds in quietly.

The room is engulfed in a sudden silence. It's as if we all have some mutual agreement to not talk about what happened between Blake and me because no one says anything else as we start to work on our assignments. We stay up for as long as we can until we can barely keep our eyes open and decide to call it a night.

The next morning, the girls and I decide to spend the day in since we don't have any classes and it's way too cold outside to do much of anything. We're halfway through our movie when there's a knock on the door.

"Are you guys expecting anybody?" I ask and they shake their heads as I get up to answer it.

"Hi—" I start to greet but it's as if the words are stuck in my mouth when I see who's standing in the hallway.

Blake Harper looks nothing like he did when I last saw him. He's even leaner and more toned than before, and even through the turtleneck he has on, I can see exactly how defined his muscles have gotten. His hair is tousled and messy in a cute way. The facial hair he seemingly decided to grow out makes him seem more attractive than I thought possible. He flashes me his signature smirk as he leans on the doorframe. The butterflies I haven't felt in months make a sudden appearance, and my heart feels like it's going to burst out of my chest.

"Blake," I finally manage to get out. "What are you doing here?"

He steps so close to me that I can feel the heat of his body on mine. He tucks a loose strand of hair behind my ear and leaves his hand cupped around my cheek.

"I'm keeping my promise." One of his arms quickly circle around my waist, pulling me closer to him as his lips crash against mine. He kisses me with such intensity and passion, it's as if he's trying to make up for all the time we've spent apart.

An exhilarating feeling courses through my body, and as I kiss Blake, I know that I can never love anyone as much as I love him. Blake is my endgame.

As we smiled against each other's lips, I know he feels the same.

Do you like YA stories?
Here are samples of other stories
you might enjoy!

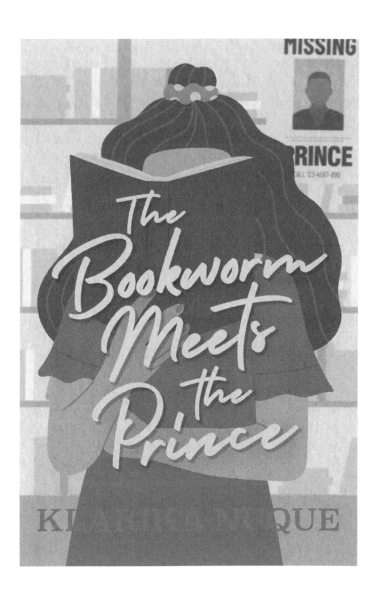

CHAPTER ONE
The Bookworm Meets the Prince

"*Just remember, my little Lizzie, no reading until you learn your lesson.*"

I knew what you'd probably be thinking, why did my dad ban me from reading? Well, everyone had their vice: mine turned out to be reading.

"*Yes, Dad. I'll try my best,*" I said over the phone.

I was completely lying, but I just couldn't help it. Though maybe as a compromise, I could tone it down to four books a week. That was me keeping my end of the bargain. That could work, right?

Book bans were the worst punishment. I meant zero access to your book collection and zero access to a book store. Could you think of anything crueler? Now I had to add going to the library on my schedule just so I could read books that were already part of my collection.

The funny thing was when I was a kid, they demanded that I had to read a certain number of books every year and a certain number of chapters every day. But when I got older and addicted to reading books, they were concerned it was all I only did and I was ruining my eyesight.

So what was the perfect solution? I was banned from buying and reading books until I learned my lesson.

"*Alright, sweetie, I have to go now. My client just arrived, and this deal might mean that I can finally buy that surprise gift for your mom,*" he said in an excited manner. *"I'll see you later and I love you, my little Lizzie."*

"Love you too, Dad," I said before ending the call.

While placing my phone inside my bag, I couldn't help but laugh a little at Dad's tricks. Fortunately, before my phone went to sleep mode, I saw the time and almost screamed. The library was closing in fifteen minutes, and there were a few books I needed to check out. So I sprinted my way to the library and made it with just ten minutes to spare.

I said a quick hello to Mel, the school librarian, before I proceeded to collect the books I wanted to read that week. I picked up *Pride and Prejudice, Sense and Sensibility, Persuasion,* and *Emma* because I decided it would be a Jane Austen week. Book bans made me sad, and you could never go wrong with Austen to cheer you up.

I was on my way to Mel to check the books out when someone suddenly bumped into me, causing my books to fall on the floor.

"What the—" I was not able to finish my sentence because I locked eyes with the most captivating blue eyes I had ever seen. The guy was so good-looking, he could be a model. He had black hair and perfectly tanned skin. For a moment, I forgot that I was in love with Mr. Darcy.

Time stood still, and I genuinely felt that we were the only two people in the whole world.

"I'm so sorry," the blue-eyed guy said. Oh my gosh! Even his voice sounded enchanting.

He then broke eye contact with me, picked up some of the books that fell and then gave them to me. After doing such, he went on his way, and for some odd reason, I got the vibe that he was running away from something or someone. Strange vibe? It was, but I guessed he was also in a hurry to pick up a book he needed like me, which reminded me of my books to check out.

"Sh*t." I quickly gathered my stuff, ran to Mel's desk, and checked out my books before they close.

"Let me guess, Lizzie. Are you banned from reading again?" Mel asked while she was encoding my books on her computer.

Melissa Daniels was not the typical scary librarian who'd shout at every person when they'd hear a noise. She was cooler than that. She actually became my friend the first time my father banned me from reading three years ago, back when I was a freshman here in Midview High.

"Yeah. Though this time, they didn't mention an end date to the punishment. This means you'll be seeing more of me in the next few weeks—hopefully not months. I already miss my babies," I said while pouting.

Today, while watching her check my books out, I was given the time to see her outfit properly. She was wearing a white blouse tucked by a black pencil skirt and a slim red belt around her waist; a typical librarian outfit, but she accessorized it with bangles and a four-inch red stiletto.

It never ceased to amaze me that she could walk and keep the library as orderly as it was in such high heels. Meanwhile, I still couldn't walk in a straight line in my flats. Every time I told her that, Mel would simply laugh and say, "It takes years of practice, Lizzie."

"Well, good luck with that, Lizzie. But if I know one thing, this is for the best. I haven't seen someone as addicted to reading as you. This might be a good opportunity for you to look beyond your books and start living in reality," she suggested while giving me the check-out receipt. I guess she had a point; I'd try and tone it down.

I waved goodbye to Mel and walked by the parking lot. I got into my Montero when I noticed something different in the parking lot: a black Lamborghini. The kids who went to Midview were well-off but were not rich enough to afford a luxury sports car. But what shocked me even more was the fact that the same blue-eyed guy who bumped into me in the library got into the expensive car. What was weirder was, he was looking around whether someone saw him going inside the car.

I wondered what he was doing here. There was no talk about a transfer student this year; that would have made the rumor mill go wild if ever. Oh well, whatever he was doing in school, he must have a purpose. It was something that shouldn't involve me because I had Austen to read when I got home.

Well, that was the plan until my phone rang. It was at times like this when I found myself thankful for Bluetooth technology.

"*Hello,*" I greeted while I was backing up the car.

"*Lizzie, I'm picking you up in exactly forty-five minutes so we can go to that party I was telling you guys about last week. So get pretty and sexy for the night, and I mean wearing contacts, not glasses,*" Rissa said on the other line.

I totally forgot about that. Rissa, my best friend on the entire planet, would always invite me to parties.

I pouted my lips while contemplating on whether I would give her the parents-can't-let-me-go or the I-have-homework excuse.

"*Uh, Rissa. The thing is—*"

She cut in before I could tell her any excuse.

"*There are no buts on this one, Lizzie. I talked to your parents and they gave me the go signal, saying that you have nothing better to do because you were banned from reading again. Plus I have the same classes as you, except for gym, and I very well know that we do not have any homework or quiz in the next few days. So yeah, I have basically ruined all your excuses. You're going to this party, and that is final. See you in forty-three minutes, and you better be dressed. See yah, beotch.*" She then hanged up.

My best friend really knew me well.

After ten minutes, I got home, had a quick shower, wore one of my black dresses, curled my hair a bit, and put some lip gloss on. If you hadn't figured out that I was hopeless in the makeup department, then yes, I was hopeless in the makeup department. It was an art I never really mastered.

I decided to wait for Rissa in the living room where I saw my mom approaching.

"Hey, Rissa told us you were going to a party tonight. Have fun, darling. It makes me so happy there is something to keep your nose out of a book tonight," my mom said while hugging me.

"You know, Mom. Some parents would die just to see their kids read a book and not go out," I pointed out while hugging her too.

"Yes, but those parents do not have a kid who spends more time reading than socializing with people. We want you to love reading, Lizzie, but we also want you to have a life. Balance is very important, and that's what we are teaching you now," my mom answered back while looking directly into my eyes.

We then heard a honking sound. Rissa just arrived. Mom accompanied me outside to say a quick hello to Rissa.

When I got into Rissa's Camry, I noticed that she already picked up Lisa and Carrie, her other friends.

"Anyone would like to tell me what this party is all about?" I asked.

"Chad wanted people to come and celebrate their football season win in his house. So that's where we're going," Rissa answered.

"You mean to say you dragged me from home to attend some high school party thrown by your quarterback boyfriend?" I asked in an irritated voice.

Rissa and Chad had been dating since sophomore year—the typical quarterback and head cheerleader drama. Well, yeah. That was them.

Rissa and I had been best friends since we were three years old, and as we grew up, we never let go of that bond even if I became a nerd and she became a cheerleader. She tried her best to keep me in her world, especially after she became the captain. Her following had to do what she said, so they tried their best to be nice or, at least, civil towards me. But the fact was, they would never accept a nerd like me to their popular clique.

As she parked her car, I noticed something on the driveway. It was the same black Lamborghini sports car I saw earlier. I wondered why it was here.

"Wow, I never knew Chad had a new car, Rissa," Lisa said.

"No, that's not Chad's car. I don't know who owns it. Maybe one of the guests does," Rissa said, who just shrugged it off.

"Well, whoever owns it must be totally loaded if he can buy a Lambo," Carrie said.

I was about to comment that I knew—no—that I saw the guy who owned the car, but Chad saw us and immediately went to greet us, especially his girlfriend.

"Hey, guys. Well, I hope you enjoy the party, but I will now snatch my girlfriend. Bye," he said after giving Rissa a kiss, and then they disappeared.

"I guess I'll see you guys later. I will go find Marco," Lisa said.

"Do you think Matt is with him? I'll go look for him too. See yah later, Liz," Carrie said.

You now know why I hated going to parties. Ever since Rissa had a boyfriend, she somewhat started ditching me during parties. She apparently wanted me to socialize with people and possibly hook up with someone who'd be too drunk to remember my name in the morning. Oh well, since I couldn't go home yet and I am here, I decided to look for a quiet spot in this mansion called Chad's home.

I went to the garden and found a lighted gazebo. It was still early and all the guests were still inside. I went inside the gazebo and sat on one of the benches. I wished I brought a book with me, but I guess technology would keep me sane until that friend of mine decided to go home. I got my phone out from my bag and started reading stories on Wattpad.

I was halfway done with the sixth chapter of the book when someone cleared his throat. I looked up and saw the same captivating blue eyes I saw in the library. He was smiling at me but seemed confused, like he was wondering what I was doing here away from the crowd. I also saw that he had this twinkle in his eye that seemed to be amazed at just seeing me in the first place. He then stood a little straighter; maximizing his height. To an ordinary person, his stance would be perceived as commanding and that all attention must be on him. I'm not sure why, but I knew that he does this when he's nervous, deep in thought, or he didn't know exactly what to do. There was just something that screams defense mechanism to it.

Well, whatever that was, one thing was for sure, he looked like he wasn't in a hurry to leave this time.

If you enjoyed this sample, look for
The Bookworm Meets the Prince
on Amazon.

try and catch me

SARAH KIRCHNER

PROLOGUE

Samantha sat across the cafeteria eating with all her friends. They were all huddled around her waiting for her to talk, like she was God, and they were her disciples. It made me gag. With every word Sam spoke, all of her friends fell further in love with her. Sam would giggle out a saying and then flick her blonde hair. And at that, everyone would swoon.

Everyone except me, that is.

I sat alone which was the usual. The three friends that I had didn't have the same lunch schedule as me, so that meant I ate alone while I watched my sister enjoy everyone's company. I hated her for being liked by everybody. She was the prettier twin. The more liked twin—not according to Quinn and Rebecca, of course—but to me it was so.

If she was the head cheerleader, which she was, I was the water girl.

I couldn't stand Sam. Ever since middle school, she has done nothing but push her way up the social ladder using her looks and charm. With her rise in popularity, you would think that I would have climbed up with her, but nothing could have been more wrong. I was stuck at the bottom, forced to endure endless torment. At school, Sam pretended as if I didn't exist. When we were home, sometimes we would hang out, but somewhere along the way, that stopped, and I was thrown to the wolves.

CHAPTER 1
Hey Sis

I hated parties.

Parties were probably my least favorite things. But Sam loved them. She threw one practically every weekend our parents went out, and this weekend was no exception.

I could already feel the bass from upstairs in my room. The floor shook beneath my feet, making it difficult for me to apply my eyeliner.

"It's only nine!" Quinn shouted from behind me. "Why is the music already blasting?" She covered her head with my pillow and fell onto the bed. "How many people can actually be here already?"

"Explain to me again. Why are we going to Sam's party?" Becca asked from the bathroom linked to my room. She was applying her makeup there since I was taking up the full-length mirror in my room.

"I'm tired of having to ditch my own house almost every Friday night," I said and threw my eyeliner into my makeup bag. I had given up applying it and decided that my brown eye shadow was good enough. I stood up and examined my outfit. It wasn't much. A black dress that hugged my skin and a flannel to cover my arms. A pair of black sneaker pumps completed my outfit. It wasn't every day I got to dress up. Usually, I just wore soccer clothes, so this was a treat.

"We could be watching America's Next Top Model right now." Quinn moaned and lifted the pillow from her face. "Did you know there's a marathon tonight?" It was clear they hated parties just as much as I did. I guess that's why we're friends

"Fine," I said, spinning around. "If you want to watch that, go ahead. I'm going downstairs," I hissed. They both looked at each other in alarm.

I flicked my blonde hair over my shoulder and strutted over to the door.

Before I could leave, the door swung open.

"Let's go party, bitches!" Caleb shouted in the doorway and ran over to my bed, landing on it with a soft thud. Caleb jumped around Quinn who sat in a ball in the middle, screaming. "We're going to a party! We're going to a party!" Caleb sang as he jumped all around. For whatever reason, he loved parties, but, unfortunately, our group never got to go to any. It was usually because Sam was there. It was already bad that I had to live in the same town as her, let alone in the same house. Caleb would always say that we should throw our own party or that we should go to more, but us nobodies never went to cool parties, so that was out of the question.

Him being six-feet tall, I was sure he was bound to hit his head on my slanted ceiling. Each time he jumped on my bed, his blond hair bounced closer to it.

"I swear, if you hit your head and die...," I began. I grabbed a towel that was hanging on my door and threw it at him. He flinched a little but continued to jump, wearing his usual goofy grin. "...I am not cleaning up your blood stains!" I shouted. Caleb only winked at me.

"That looks like fun!" Becca shouted and ran over to the bed, too. She crawled onto it and stood, holding Caleb's hands and jumping with him around a now very panicked Quinn.

"I hate you all." I sighed and turned to leave my room for the second time.

In my doorway, though, now stood the mega bitch. She glared at me with her emerald eyes. Her perfectly waxed eyebrows were pinched together. Her curled blonde hair was perfectly placed over her shoulder as she crossed her bony arms.

It was Sam.

It was my twin sister.

Yay.

"Hey sis." I smiled and leaned against the wall in the doorway. Sam frowned at me. While I just strongly disliked her, she despised me. Twins were supposed to be closer than normal siblings, but it was different for us. It seemed normal for siblings to fight, but twins? I always saw twins as siblings who'd always hang out together. They shared the same group of friends, and they always got along with each other. A twin was like a permanent best friend, but for me and Samantha, it was more like the bane of our existence.

"Ah, welcome to the real party, Samantha!" Caleb shouted from my bed. He was smiling like crazy. I wanted to laugh at his funny face, but contained it. Sam cringed upon seeing him.

"No one invited you here, Caleb." She sneered. There it was. Her nasty attitude. It was honestly amazing how people haven't caught on to her act yet.

But then, I remembered it was only when she was around me and my friends that we saw the horrific side of the mega bitch. Whenever she was with her friends, she turned into an angel automatically. No, no that wasn't the right word. She became a goddess.

Caleb laughed and pounced off the bed. He snuck closer to her and placed his hands on her hips. Sam tensed up right away. Caleb licked his lips and leaned toward her ear. "Oh, but didn't you invite me?" he whispered. Caleb loved teasing Sam, and that made me love him even more.

Sam elbowed him in the stomach. Caleb chuckled as he backed off. "In case you missed it Caleb, I have a boyfriend." She glared at both of us, but we were too busy laughing to care.

Caleb waved Sam away and went back over to my bed.

"Can I help you with something?" I asked Sam.

"It sounds like you guys are having a threesome from downstairs," she growled. She glanced over my shoulder and noticed my other friends in the room. "Well, in this case, maybe it was a foursome." She snickered at her clever comeback. Hilarious.

Caleb laughed and put his arms around Quinn and Becca on the bed. "Want to join us, Sam?" he asked her, raising an eyebrow. "I'm sure we can all fit." He winked. Quinn and Becca giggled.

Sam scoffed with disgust after giving us an eye roll. "Just keep it down." She gave us each one last glare before strutting down the hallway and down the stairs. If looks could kill, we would have all been dead by now.

"Does she know we're actually coming to the party this time?" Becca said.

"Who cares?" I laughed and grabbed Becca's and Quinn's hands. "Let's go have some fun!" I squealed, and we paraded through the door.

"This is gonna be epic!" Caleb shouted from behind us, throwing his hands up. The girls and I laughed at his comment and descended the white stairs.

That's when the party hit me—the pungent smell of cheap liquor, weed, and sweat infiltrating my nose. In our living room was a guy I faintly knew. His name was Eric, and he was the DJ for the night. EDM blasted through the speakers that were placed strategically around the house so every corner boomed with the music. In the room with Eric was a swarm of kids dancing, rubbing their bodies against each other. Guys nibbled at girls' ears, while the girls giggled and swayed back and forth.

Quinn practically threw up right away.

"I think I'm gonna get sick." She covered her mouth and ran back up the stairs. My eyes locked with Becca's. Becca just tossed her hair over her shoulder and jumped off the last step.

"Let her be. We're here to have fun." She smiled and danced her way through the crowd, her red hair bobbing up and down as she moved.

Caleb smiled as Becca began dancing in the center of the dance floor.

"That girl's wild." He chuckled.

"Oh yeah?" I said and took a look at him. His eyes were bright. "Why don't you go dance with her?" I nudged him a couple times in the stomach and gave him some winks.

"No, I... uh...," Caleb stuttered and scratched his head. "That's not who I want to dance with, Ella." He coughed and glanced at his feet.

"Okay, whatever." I rolled my eyes and left Caleb on the stairs. "I'm going to get a drink."

"Wait! Ella!" he called and tried to come with me.

"Go to Rebecca!" I shouted back and headed into the kitchen.

The kitchen didn't have many people in it. Just a couple making out near our fridge. It was gross, but that's what happened at parties. People got drunk, and other people hooked up.

I looked at the island and saw the drink options: beer, vodka, and Coke. Both the beer and vodka smelled revolting, so I played it safe and chose the soda. Besides, I wanted to attend my first party sober. I grabbed a can and flicked it open. Immediately, soda began pouring out, spraying its contents all over the white kitchen. *Crap.* I turned and tried to run to the sink before I made a mess. Well, I tried to, at least.

Before I could get two feet from where the soda began exploding, I ran into a body. A male body. Brown soda soaked the white shirt he wore, and his shirt now stuck to him. That's when I noticed the amazing six pack on the guy I just bumped into.

"I'm so sorry!" I squeaked and grabbed a towel that hung on the stove. I began dabbing his stomach, making myself look like a bigger idiot than I already am. "Oh my god, your shirt is probably ruined," I groaned and covered my head.

"Relax, Sam. It's totally okay." The guy laughed and grabbed my wrists.

I froze. My eyes slammed shut. He thought I was Sam. This guy with rocking abs thought I was my twin sister. My better and prettier twin sister.

The guy lowered my hands and I snuck a peek at the guy. My breath caught in my throat.

It was Aspen.

It was freaking Aspen-totally hot-Carder.

He was the star of the championship soccer team at our school. He played forward and scored three out of the four goals at the game. He was tall with adorable curly brown hair, which was hanging loosely around his ears right now. He looked amazing causing my heart to race. I couldn't believe I had spilt my drink all over the star athlete.

"Oh! Ella!" he exclaimed and quickly let go of my hands. "Sorry, I... um... I saw the blonde hair and..." he explained, gesturing at my head. "And I thought you were your sister." His face was turning red. *Was he embarrassed?* He was probably scared to be seen with me. People usually wanted to be with my sister, not me.

I shrugged and tried to hide my face. "Everyone does," I mumbled.

We stood there in an awkward silence. I waited for him to say something, but he just stared at me with his chocolate eyes. A small smile spread on his lips.

"Aspen!" A girl squealed from the sliding glass door. We both jumped and looked to see who it was.

Sam.

"Silly, that's not me!" She laughed and skipped over to him. Her arm snaked under his, linking arms with him.

"Hi, Sam." I put on the smile that I always did when she was around. "Where's James?" I asked.

James Smith was her boyfriend. They had been dating since last year, around Homecoming. Of course, they were declared the sophomore Homecoming king and queen. Now it was a new year, and Homecoming was in two months. There was no way she would dump James before then. It was always expected that the captain of the cheerleading squad dated the quarterback of the football team.

"Ella, why don't you just go back to your room? You do hate parties, don't you?" She put on a smile as well and turned to Aspen. "Now, come on, Aspen. We're having a soccer game out back, and I already declared you captain."

It was sickening how sweet and nice she tried to be with Aspen. Clearly, she had a crush on him, and if she really wanted him, she could get him. It didn't make sense why she was with James. Both James and Aspen were amazing athletes. Aspen was better than James, but...

Sam nodded toward the fenced-in backyard. A soccer ball was bouncing between some teenagers. They were all mostly from the guys soccer team. I didn't see any girls playing.

"Cool." He nodded and began heading for the door.

"Wait, you're playing soccer?" I asked before Sam left the kitchen. She scrunched her eyebrows at me.

"Oh, yeah. Ella, you play right?" Aspen asked, his head tilted in my direction. "You should totally play with us."

My heart skipped a beat.

"Yeah," I said, smirking at Sam. "I would love to play."

If you enjoyed this sample, look for
Try and Catch Me

on Amazon.

PROLOGUE

I looked at my reflection with dull eyes while drops of water were dripping from my hair. The steam from the shower was fogging the mirror, but I could still see myself through it. I sometimes thought that maybe, just maybe, one day I would see a different person with happiness and confidence.

I looked in the mirror to see my flaws that I have grown to accept. The flaws everyone used against me, but why should I care?

Yes, I could be a better person. I could walk to school every day with so much confidence that would bring everyone to their knees.

But why haven't I done that yet? Why did I keep on staring at myself every morning as if it would make things better or make a difference for everyone to like me?

My chubby cheeks and fat belly were one of the reasons why nobody liked me. I was the chipmunk of the whole middle school. I would walk around while everyone called me names, emphasizing why I stood out so much.

It had been like this since elementary school. Probably because I was not much of an active person. I would usually stay home all day and watch TV. I didn't like most things except eating. I mean, who wouldn't? It helped ease the stress. My dad owned a pizza shop that was quite known in our little town of Strawberry Forest in California.

Yes, I knew it was a weird name. Our town was known for growing strawberries in the old days that covered our land like a forest.

I used to go to his pizza place every Friday just to have a bite of heaven, which was probably another reason why I became chubby.

I wrapped the towel tighter around my body as I let my short, straight hair fall down to my shoulders.

I really needed to let it grow.

Walking out of the bathroom, I then headed to my closet. I grabbed a pair of baggy jeans and my favorite sweatshirt that my mom bought me on my twelfth birthday. My fashion sense was another thing I needed to fix.

But should I really care about what everyone would think of how I dress?

I put the clothes on, let my wet hair fall down naturally, and climbed down the stairs to smell the scent of my mom's amazing pancakes. I inhaled it happily and skipped towards the kitchen to see my dad sitting down, reading a book while my mom works at the stove.

My dad was the first to notice me and gave me a smile as he put his book down. He then motioned me to come over.

"Good morning, pumpkin," my dad said, catching my mom's attention. She put the pancake she had on the pan into a plate and turned the stove off. She wiped her hands on the towel next to her and turned to look at me.

"Good morning, mom and dad," I said as I kissed each of them on the cheek. I then grabbed the chair next to my dad and sat down, licking my lips as I stared at the plate in front of me with hungry eyes.

"Is my little girl excited to finish school today?" my mom asked.

Who wouldn't be? School was a living hell because of the constant bullying from none other than Tyl—

No! I promised myself I would never bring up his name as long as I'm alive!

Okay, maybe I was exaggerating a bit. Could you blame me when everyone constantly picked on me just because of how I looked, especially if it was only because one person started it?

"Mom, I'm not a little girl anymore." I groaned playfully as I cut a little piece of my pancake and shoved it in my mouth. The delicious taste in my mouth made me want to moan.

My mom took a seat in front of me and smiled as she pinched my cheek.

"Oh, but you'll always be my little girl," she said, attracting my father's attention. He put his book down again and glared at my mom.

"Hey, that's my line," he said.

I rolled my eyes at them, knowing what they were about to start.

My mom leaned against the table as she put her fist under her chin and smiled teasingly.

"Well, I stole it. *Whatcha* going to do about it?" She teased.

"Why, you!" my dad said.

That was my cue to look away. I ate my breakfast quickly before it got cold. It was obvious that I preferred to watch the pancakes over my parents smooching.

I ignored my parents' little playful argument which would lead to a make out season right here in front of me because trust me, it would always make me want to gag. I finished my plate and placed it in the sink. I turned around and found my parents eating each other's faces.

Ew, couldn't they get a room?

"Mom." I whined.

"Dad!" I said a bit louder and heard a knock at the front door.

"I'll get it," I muttered and headed to the door. I looked through the peephole and smiled when I saw who it was. I opened it and jumped into my best friend's arms as I ruffled his hair and messed it up.

I pulled away and smiled seeing Matt's annoyed face. He was probably the only reason I wake up every morning to go to school. He was practically my rock who was always there for me when I needed a shoulder to cry on, and defended me from all the bullying.

It wasn't like he could stop it in general, but his presence would help me cope with it.

We met somewhere in elementary school and clicked instantly. Matt was like the big brother I never had, supporting me through both the ups and the downs.

"What?" I asked with a smirk. He glared at me and pointed at his hair.

"Really? It takes me forever to fix this." He whined as he tried to fix his hair. Sometimes, I thought he cared about his looks more than I cared about mine.

I grinned and shrugged my shoulders.

"Oh, don't be such a grouch! It's the last day of school, lighten up," I said, punching his shoulder. He gave me a small smile and nodded his head.

"Are you ready?" he asked.

"Yeah, just give me a second," I said and ran back into the kitchen. "Mom, dad, I'm leaving." They smiled and engulfed me a big hug and wished me good luck.

My parents knew that I was being picked on, but they didn't really know that I was being bullied every single day by Ty—

No! Not again.

As I was saying, I thought it was best that they didn't know for them not to worry. Besides, they have already reported it to the principal countless times, but nothing happened. It just wouldn't stop.

I went to the front door where Matt was waiting and closed it behind me. The chill of the morning hit my face as the breeze quickened. It was still early, about seven something, but classes wouldn't start until eight.

I was actually excited to finish this day without problems. Matt and I walked to the school which wasn't too far away and talked about summer. Time went by quickly and the next thing I knew, I was in front of the place I hated the most. I started walking down the hall with Matt at my side as I tried to ignore everyone including the snickers made by some girls hanging by their lockers. As long as I wouldn't bump into him today, I would be fine.

When the bell rang, I sprinted out of my seventh period class and down the hall to head to the school gates at the edge of the school's parking lot. I would usually head towards that direction to meet Matt and walk home together afterwards. Surprisingly, this day just went by simply. I mean, I got called with names a few times, but there was nothing new. I guess everyone was too busy to go home from school and begin their summer vacation, so I wasn't their priority today.

Matt and I usually took our lunch together, and as I went between my classes, I would hide in the mass of children who were bumping into each other to avoid being spotted by my enemy.

Luck was on my side for not seeing him today. I stepped out of the door at the end of the hallway, walked to the parking lot, and looked around for Matt but couldn't see him. I assumed that I was early so I waited under a tree that was planted on the side of the gate. After all, it wasn't the first time he was late.

Suddenly, my vision blurred as something cold hit my head. I squealed in surprise and wrapped my arms around me. When I opened my eyes, I heard laughter echoing through the air and found myself soaking wet.

I wiped the water blurring my vision and looked up in the branches to see two boys, holding empty buckets and laughing their butts off. I was embarrassed, and I felt tears run through my cheeks, but I held them back.

Why would they do this to me? All I wanted was to go home and forget about the worst seven hours of my life that I had to repeat five times a week. All I wanted was to have a normal life like everyone else.

I pushed those thoughts away and was about to shout at the boys when someone else called my name. Shivers ran down my spine as I feared what I was about to face.

Taking a deep breath, I looked upon the face that I hated the most—the one who made my life a living hell.

Tyler Grey was holding something in his hand which I thought a water balloon.

"Just a little reminder of me throughout your summer," he said with a smirk, and threw the balloon at me before I could even move.

Paint. It was paint.

The boys up in the tree climbed down and walked over to Tyler. They were barely able to contain themselves from laughing and gave him a pat on the back. It was then that I could no longer control the tears in my eyes from running down my cheeks. I saw Tyler's eyes glaring at me, and clenched my fists as I watched them walk away with taunting smiles as if they had just won the lottery.

I took a shaky breath as the tears blurred my vision. My day spiraled from ten all the way to a zero because of him. I was freaking wet and my favorite grey sweatshirt now turned pink. I fell to the ground as I sobbed with my knees on my chest and hid my head.

I heard Matt call out from a distance, but I didn't pay attention. My mind was clogged and overflowing with hateful thoughts toward Tyler Grey.

My eyes were blinded from any light that I could have seen. My ears were plugged with his words. He got what he wanted; I was never going to forget him this summer. His face would forever haunt my mind.

CHAPTER 1

I stepped out of the taxi and paid the driver his tip. My long, tan legs resembled like hotdogs that were being heated under the bright, shining sun. I pulled the sunglasses away from my eyes and rested them on my head, looking around the place I used to call home where I lived many years ago.

Once I was completely alone in the quiet, familiar streets, I made my way to the house, and could instantly tell that not much had changed. The grass was as green as ever, and the birds were flying from branch to branch. It was as if I had never left. Although, it did look like it needed some dusting and a few plants in the front yard. But other than that, everything was fine.

I had argued with myself countless times about whether to buy a new house or just come back to this place. My childhood wasn't quite the best, but I would always choose my heart's desire. It wanted to go back home—to the place where I was raised.

I decided to come back to this small town everyone called Strawberry Forest. Was going back to the same house that hold good yet disturbing memories a good idea? Would I enjoy my life here? Or would I just end up regretting my decision?

I walked to the front door and stared at it for what seemed to be hours but were only seconds. Was I ready to face the past? Coming back here after so many years could be a good thing. I may had been away for so long, but it wasn't enough to help me erase and forget the dreadful memories of what this house and town gave me. Nevertheless, I couldn't exactly stop now. I was here for a reason, and that was to stop running away. I had to face reality.

I looked around to see that the house next to us was a bit different than I remembered. Its paint was in a different color and had a different vibe radiating from it. The decorations were of a different taste than that of the previous owner.

New neighbors perhaps?

I finally gathered all the courage that I had and grabbed the keys in my pocket. I opened the door and it creaked as I opened it slowly. Dust flew in the air as the house had not been touched for years. I took a step into the house, and looked around to see memories of the past flood my mind.

The interior and furniture were untouched. I didn't want anything removed when I moved away. I didn't even let my grandma sell it, knowing that I would be back one day.

I closed the door and realized that I would need help in cleaning this place; I didn't think I could do it alone. I grabbed my phone from my bag to send my best friend a text message on my arrival, telling him that I would be expecting his presence in a couple of minutes. I rubbed my eyes to prevent the tears from falling. I was done running away and was going to start a new life now that I had returned. A life that would make my parents proud.

* * *

Three years ago

I walked up to the front door as I wiped the water off my face with the napkin Matt gave me. Matt had been furious throughout the entire walk. He was ranting about how people could be so cruel, especially on the last day of school. Well, we were talking about Tyler Grey so I wasn't surprised.

He also blamed himself for being late. In his mind, if he was there sooner then maybe he could have prevented it. I disagreed and told him that it was fine. My life had been like this for years so I was pretty used to it.

After saying our 'goodbyes' a couple of blocks away, I stood right outside the front door, too afraid to face my parents. What would they say if they saw me like this? They would definitely freak out.

What would I tell them?

I could just lie and say that it was a goodbye prank from a couple of friends. Or, that there was this activity in school where we fought with water balloons. But of course, that would be such a lame lie, and they would not believe me. They knew me too well, and would be suspicious of the pink paint that stained all over my sweatshirt.

I decided to just tell them the truth and get it over with.

I rang the doorbell, waiting for the door to open. Moments passed as I stared at the door and rang the doorbell again, assuming they may have just not heard the first attempt. I waited another minute or two until I figured out no one was going to open the door. I rolled my eyes and guessed that my parents were probably up in their room making out because this wasn't the first time they've been getting it on while I waited outside.

Sighing, I grabbed the pot that had a plant in it and dug for the emergency key to open the door. I walked in to see no one. I took the risk of going upstairs to my parents' room and was surprised to hear nothing and thought that maybe they have fallen asleep.

Pft, come on. Who sleeps at this time?

I knocked on the door and waited for an answer, but nothing happened. I knocked again but this time, I opened the door to stare at nothing. There was no one in the room. It was completely empty as if it haven't been touched since I had left for school.

I ran down stairs to the kitchen and saw that my mom haven't made dinner at all. Well, that was strange. My parents used to leave something for me to eat before going somewhere else. It wasn't that I was always hungry; I just found it strange.

I walked into the living room and grabbed the house phone. I dialed my mom's number, but no one answered. I dialed dad's number, but he didn't answer either.

I was just about to go upstairs to my room when the doorbell rang. I skipped toward the front door thinking it might be them. When I peeped through the peephole, it wasn't my parents standing outside but two men wearing police uniforms.

I opened the door and stared up at the strangers who were standing in front of me, both of whom gave me sympathetic looks for some unknown reason. I lifted an eyebrow in confusion.

"Can I help you officers?"

They both glanced at each other then looked at me.

"You must be Crystal Clare," one of them said.

I nodded my head slowly, wondering why and how they knew my name.

"Yes, that's me. Is there something wrong?" I asked nervously.

"Yes. Unfortunately, your parents were in an accident, and we need to take you to the police station for some information."

My eyes widened, and my heart started to beat so fast that I could feel it hitting my chest. I felt a lump form in my throat as his words sunk into my brain and my world started to spin.

"An accident?" I gasped softly.

I felt tears form in my eyes, and my palms began to sweat.

"Are they okay?" I asked.

I couldn't imagine living without my parents. They were one of the reasons I stayed positive in life. They were amazingly supportive and always gave me warm hugs when I needed them.

If something were to happen to them, then I would be in this life all on my own. I didn't have anyone else here in this small town to take care of me. My life would become way worse than it already was.

One of the policemen took off the cap he was wearing and looked down at me with tender eyes, shaking his head.

"I'm sorry for your loss," he said.

After hearing those words, I couldn't stop the tears from flowing. My parents were dead.

* * *

I snapped out of my thoughts when I heard the doorbell rang. I took the sunglasses off my head, placed them on the counter, walked over to the front door, and took my shoes off. I looked through the peephole and smiled.

I quickly yanked the door open only to face the sight of Matt holding a broom.

"Matt!"

I jumped into his arms, causing him to drop the broom as he wrapped his arms around my waist. He picked me up off the ground, and our laughter filled the air.

He put me down on my feet and smiled, showing me his straight white teeth. He then looked at me from head to toe and whistled as he gave me a wolf grin.

I laughed as I punched his shoulder playfully.

"Oh my god! It's been ages," I said, letting him in before closing the door behind me.

"Yeah, I know, right? How have you been?" he asked.

"I've been good. What about you?"

It's been a very long time since I've seen Matt. But ever since I've moved to my grandparents' house in New York four years ago, we have been keeping in touch by using *Facebook* and *FaceTime*. Later on, I bought my own phone, and we called each other every day.

"Better now that you're here," he answered, as we walked toward the living room.

"You look the same like I never left," I said.

He still looked and felt like the Matt I knew many years ago, except that he had grown much taller and broader with facial hair.

"You...well, you look—"

"Different?" I asked.

He shook his head and gave me a smile wrapping his arm around my shoulders.

"Beautifuler," he said.

"That's not even a word, idiot." I chuckled, punching his shoulder again.

"It is for me," he said.

I smiled at his compliment.

Now, don't get me wrong. It wasn't like in the past four years I've been trying to change myself and get skinnier so that everyone would like me. No, that's not what happened.

I got depressed when my parents died and lived in a place I'm not familiar with. I had to meet new people which I wasn't a big fan of, but I found a solution to deal with it.

No, it wasn't drugs or alcohol. It was exercise. I would go out for a run and feel free. I wouldn't stop until I was panting for air and soaked all my clothes with my own sweat.

Doing the same routine every day, running became a hobby and made me into how I looked today.

"I hope you're ready because this place needs some cleaning," I said, as I grabbed his broom and threw it at him.

"Some?" he asked, as he grabbed the broom. "You mean, a lot. This place hasn't been touched in ages."

I cleaned the kitchen while Matt got to work in the living room. My house didn't seem huge when I lived here with my parents. We had two bedrooms upstairs and a bathroom. But now that I was going to live here all alone, it seemed so big and lonely.

I thought about it a lot and came to a conclusion that I wouldn't be moving out anytime soon. This place was sentimental, and I couldn't just let it go. I was pretty sure this was what my parents would have wanted, and I booked the nearest flight ticket to return home, the minute I turned eighteen. I've been planning that ever since I've left.

I was never close to my grandparents. I appreciated them for taking me in though, but I knew that once I turn eighteen, I'd be on my own.

After an hour and a half later, Matt and I were done cleaning the first floor. I walked out of the bathroom after cleaning myself up and saw Matt in the kitchen drinking some water.

"Let's take a break and have something to eat. I'm pretty sure you're hungry," he said.

I watched as Matt took his phone out and ordered pizza. I took two cups and a bottle of *Pepsi* to the living room and placed them on the coffee table in front of the couch. I sat down and grabbed my phone out since the TV wasn't working, and it needed some fixing with the wires and stuff.

Matt walked into the room and sat next to me. We spent time talking about everything that happened in the past four years and how the people at school were sorry for me and my loss. I wasn't planning on holding grudges against anyone, but I could never forget what they have done to me.

I told him about New York and how awesome it was. But I guess I was just a Californian girl who could never trade California for any city. I was born here after all.

Twenty minutes later, a knock was heard on the door. Matt got up to open it while I sipped on the Pepsi I had in my hand. I wasn't such a big fan of soda and preferred juice more, but there wasn't any in the fridge at the moment. I needed to buy groceries.

Matt came back with a box of pizza in his hand. I licked my lips as my stomach grumbled in hunger. When the box was opened, we dug in and ate until we were full. We pretty much finished the box, but you can't blame us. It's been a long day.

We sat in silence, gathering our thoughts until Matt spoke.

"You ready for school on Monday?" he asked.

I sighed. I knew this topic was going to be brought up. Besides, I still had to go to school.

I wished I could delay the time of me having to go to school sooner.

"Yeah," I said, nodding my head. Let's just hope that some things have changed while I was gone.

If you enjoyed this sample, look for
Tyler's Gem
on Amazon.

ACKNOWLEDGEMENTS

First and foremost, thank you to my Lord and Savior Jesus Christ for allowing me to grow and the experiences that prompted me to start putting pen to paper. Thank You for leading me and helping me become who I am today.

Huge thank you to my best friend and sister, Diana, who spent countless months helping me write this book when I needed the motivation or when I couldn't find the words. This book would be nothing without you.

Thank you to my online community of readers who have shown me nothing but love and support and push me to continue writing.

Lastly, a huge thank you to everyone at BLVNP who have been so patient with me and an amazing support system during this process. Thank you for making all of my publishing dreams come true.

AUTHOR'S NOTE

Thank you so much for reading *Say You Won't Let Go*! I can't express how grateful I am for reading something that was once just a thought inside my head.

Please feel free to send me an email. Just know that my publisher filters these emails. Good news is always welcome.
mia_golding@awesomeauthors.org

I'd love to hear your thoughts on the book. Please leave a review on Amazon or Goodreads because I just love reading your comments and getting to know you!

Can't wait to hear from you!

Mia Golding

ABOUT THE AUTHOR

Mia Golding was born and raised in Florida and fell in love with books at a very young age. She's always dreamed of being an author and finally decided to write at the age of fourteen. Her dream is now coming true at the age of eighteen! She is focused on finishing high school and going to university to study English and Creative Writing and can't wait to start writing more in the future.

Made in the USA
Middletown, DE
20 July 2021

44518716R00139